Sam doesn't like gods. They're arrogant and look at humans as if they're beneath them, and maybe they are, but Sam has no problem letting them know what he thinks of them. He tries to stay away from them as much as possible, but it's not always easy, since he works as a bartender at a trendy club.

Loki is used to people throwing themselves at him, be they humans or gods. Right now, he has too much on his mind to bother with any of them, what with his family members killing each other. Gods have always brought trouble, and his nephew Baldur's death isn't any different.

When Loki meets Sam, he can't stay away, and no matter how much Sam tries to resist, he finds himself falling for the god, something he'd promised himself he'd never do. Things between them are going well, but the same can't be said for the world around them, especially Loki's family. Will they be enough to make Sam give up and push Loki away? Or will he be able to hold onto that love and maybe be the unlikely savior Loki needs?

Unlikely Savior
Copyright © 2022 Catherine Lievens
ISBN: 978-1-4874-3543-1
Cover art by Angela Waters

Published by eXtasy Books Inc

Look for us online at:
www.eXtasybooks.com

Unlikely Savior
For the Gods' Amusement 3

By

Catherine Lievens

Chapter One

Loki couldn't avoid looking at Jimmy. It was stupid, and he knew it, but he'd really thought he and Jimmy could have something. It wasn't like him, but then, Jimmy wasn't the kind of guy Loki usually went for. He was nice and gentle, and he wanted forever, which he now had with Qebui.

And Loki had nothing.

"You're out of sorts," Nu said from beside Loki.

Loki plastered a smile on his face, not wanting his old friend to find out what he was thinking about. They were sneaky, and they'd get everything out of him if he wasn't careful. "Just a bit worried."

"Does it have anything to do with that family emergency you had?"

Nu understood family emergencies. They were one of the oldest gods in their pantheon, and they had their fingers in every situation, or so it seemed. Loki was pretty sure they knew everything that happened in their palace and that the only reason they stayed out of most of the fights was that they just couldn't be bothered.

Loki understood. Most days, it felt too much for him to deal with his family, and he didn't even live in Asgard. Usually, people went to Odin when they had a problem, but this time, Odin was right in the middle of it.

Loki shook his head. "Can we please not talk about it? I don't even want to *think* about it, to be honest." Because it was a mess, and while he'd tried, he doubted there was anything he could do to smooth things over. He'd have to continue trying, because otherwise things would become worse, and when gods were involved, that could mean anything, but for now, he wanted to focus on this family dinner.

He looked around the table. This *was* a family dinner, no matter how strange it might look from the outside. With his pale skin and leather pants, Loki didn't belong, but he wasn't the only one. Jimmy had lived in the United States until recently, but he'd integrated himself and looked at home. What was surprising was that Nu had left their palace to come down to the human one. Loki couldn't remember the last time they'd done that beyond official ceremonies, and it could only mean that they wanted to spend more time with Jimmy and Merry, who were both human. They could have gone up to the sky palace, as Jimmy called it, but clearly, Nu wanted to stay away from it.

Nu patted Loki's knee. "But remember that if you need anyone to talk to, you can come to me. I, more than anyone else, can understand what it's like to deal with a family like yours."

Loki forced himself to smile, then turned his attention back to his plate. The king had gone all out for this dinner, but then it made sense. He was meeting his consort's great-great-great-something-grandparent, and he wanted to make a good impression. Loki wanted to tell him he didn't have to and that Nu already loved him and everyone else around the table, but it wasn't his place.

What *was* his place? It wasn't in Asgard, and it wasn't in the human world. It wasn't exactly here, surrounded by Egyptian gods.

Loki had never really had a place, but he could see himself becoming more comfortable with visiting, even without being with Jimmy. The only thing he wanted was for Jimmy to be happy, and he was — much more than he could ever have been with Loki.

Loki wasn't a relationship kind of person. He had fun, lots

of sex, then disappeared and never visited the people he'd slept with again. He wouldn't have been able to do that with Jimmy. So in a way, he was glad they'd never gone beyond a date. He was pretty sure Qebui was glad for that, too. He wasn't holding a grudge, but he clearly wasn't as happy with Loki as he'd been before.

Loki didn't care. Qebui should have gotten his head out of his ass much sooner, and if he had, Loki wouldn't have taken Jimmy on a date.

But meeting Jimmy had made Loki think, and he was never comfortable when that happened. He didn't do relationships, but watching Jimmy and Qebui together made him wonder what it could be like. What if he, too, had someone to go home to at night? It was good enough for Jimmy and Qebui, so why couldn't it be for him? He'd always avoided it because it was better to stay away from complications, especially considering his family, but maybe it was time to ignore them for a while and focus a bit on himself and what he truly wanted in life.

Something brushed against his leg, and he looked down to find Nu's cat making eight figures around his ankles. He'd been surprised to find the mummified animal was there, especially with Loki the dog hanging around, but neither of them seemed to have a problem with the other. The dog was wary of the cat and kept his distance, but the cat loved the attention, so Loki leaned down and gave his bandaged head a scratch.

When he looked up, it was to see Jimmy and Qebui kissing. It wasn't sexual, which made the situation worse as far as Loki was concerned. If what Jimmy and Qebui had was just sex, he wouldn't be jealous. Instead, there was true love and care in the kiss, as if it was something they did just because they wanted to and because it was nice to tell the other they loved him. It made Loki look away, but he couldn't stop thinking about it, and after a moment, he got to his feet.

Everyone turned to look at him.

Loki was shameless, so he wasn't embarrassed by the attention. He grinned, and even though he knew the smile was lackluster, he was pretty sure the others didn't realize that. He raked a hand through his hair, pushing it away from his face, and smiled.

"I apologize, but I have to go."

Jimmy frowned. "Already? Is it the thing with your family?"

Loki hadn't told anyone what was going on with his family, and he wasn't about to now. He was sorry he was involved in it, and he didn't want anyone else to be. He didn't have a choice, but they did, and he'd be damned if he'd pull them into the mess.

Still, he couldn't exactly tell the people around the table that he was feeling maudlin and that he couldn't stand to stare at their happiness for much longer. "It is."

"Bullshit," Nu grumbled, but thankfully, they didn't call out Loki beyond that.

Loki was pretty sure that the next time he came around, they'd corner him and force him to talk, but that was a problem for the Loki of the future. Loki of the present wanted nothing more than to leave, and Loki listened to what that Loki wanted.

"Thank you again for the very nice dinner and for including me," he said, bowing slightly. "I'm sure I'll see all of you soon."

"You better," Jimmy said. "I've been worried about you, and I want to know what's going on. If you need help with anything, you can always come to us."

It still bewildered Loki that a human felt that way about him, but then he'd treated Jimmy very differently than he usually treated humans. Jimmy seemed to see something good in him that Loki himself couldn't see, and while it was touching, it was also confusing and a bit scary.

"Of course," he said with a smile that felt more natural.

He stepped away from the table, had to lean down to pat the heads of both the dog and the cat, and then, finally, he could leave. He didn't miss the way both Qebui and Nu stared at him as he walked away, but he didn't dare look back. Eventually they'd demand an explanation, and he wasn't sure what he'd do then. Yes, he considered them his family more than the gods who lived in Asgard had ever been, but that didn't mean he could burden them with what was happening.

He breathed in and out a few times once he was in the palace garden. He could have left right from the dining room, but he wanted to see this place first. For some reason, he loved it, even though it was so very different from the place where he was born. Everything here was warm, both in temperature and sights. It was a good home, but it wasn't Loki's.

He put his hands on his hips and shook his head. He might not be in a relationship, and he might not know what to do with his sudden willingness to have one, but he could still have fun. He was still Loki, and he knew exactly where to go in order to prove that to himself.

Samuel put the glass containing a cocktail and a bottle of water on the bar in front of him. "Here you go," he said. He had to raise his voice so the woman on the other side could hear him.

She turned around, saw the drinks, and smiled. She leaned forward, pressing her breasts into the counter, possibly so that Samuel would get a better look at them. Samuel could have told her he didn't care about boobs, but instead, he kept his focus on her face.

"I've been told this club is a place where gods often visit—

is it?" she asked.

Samuel almost sighed. It wasn't the first time someone asked him, and his answer would be the same as it always was. "I wouldn't call them regular. They come around sometimes, though."

It was enough to satisfy her, and she stepped away from the bar with a smile on her face. Samuel realized that most of the people came here to get a peek of the gods, but he could have done without it. He hadn't seen any of the gods yet, but he knew that eventually he would. The only reason he hadn't was that he'd just started working here a few weeks ago, but his boss had been clear when he'd told him how to behave if a god ever came around. Samuel was to give them whatever they wanted, when they wanted, and to put them before any human customer they had. That bothered Samuel, but considering his boss was the one signing his paychecks, he'd have to obey when the time came.

He just hoped it wouldn't be anytime soon.

Of course, he was wrong. About half an hour later, there was a commotion near the entrance. It got the attention of Samuel and the other two bartenders who worked behind the counter, and Samuel held his breath, wondering if a fight had broken out. It wouldn't be the first nor the last, but he was relieved to see that tonight that wasn't the case, at least until he realized what *had* happened.

A tall man strode into the club.

Samuel didn't have to ask who it was. He was very much aware of Loki, and he was pretty sure everyone in the club was. All gazes were instantly on the god, even Samuel's, no matter how little he liked it. He felt as if he couldn't look away, but it wasn't just because Loki was a god and his power almost crackled on his skin.

Loki was gorgeous. Samuel had seen pictures, but that hadn't prepared him for the real thing. As Loki strode toward the bar, he couldn't look away. The god was as tall as Samuel, but where Samuel was broad and muscled, Loki was thin, almost as if a strong gust of wind would be enough to send him to the ground. His long black hair hung around his face, and his dark eyes sparkled as he leaned against the counter. His skin was much lighter than Samuel's, even though Samuel was blond with blue eyes. He tanned easily, but Loki looked like he hadn't spent one day in the sun.

Samuel cleared his throat and straightened his back. He plastered a smile on his face, berated himself for thinking about Loki that way, and leaned forward.

"Can I get you anything?"

Loki cocked his head as he stared. "You're new," he said.

It wasn't a question, but Samuel nodded anyway. "I am. So? Can I get you anything?"

"I'll get your usual," one of Samuel's colleagues said.

He turned to glare at her, but she wasn't looking at him anymore. She'd already turned to grab whatever Loki's usual was.

Samuel supposed that meant he wouldn't have to worry about the god, so he turned to move on to other customers. The god was in good hands, which meant Samuel was free to continue doing his job. He served drinks for several more people, and all of them kept staring at Loki, who was now holding a glass of something dark and sipping on it as he stared at Samuel. He wasn't even trying to hide it, for fuck's sake.

What did he expect Samuel to do? Fall all over himself so he could get Loki whatever he was drinking? Well, if that was what the god had expected, he had to be sorely disappointed. Samuel didn't lick anyone's boots, not even Loki's.

But it would probably be a good idea not to be too antagonizing. His boss had been clear when he'd told him what to do in the event gods visited, and while Samuel had done everything he had to, he was on the edge of not being polite. He was relieved the other two bartenders had Loki in hand and were serving him every time he wiggled his fingers at them. Loki never tried to get Samuel to come closer, which Samuel was more than happy with.

The problem was that no matter how hard he tried to ignore the god, part of him was hyper-focused on his presence. He kept peeking in that direction, even though he told himself he shouldn't every time it happened. It was even more infuriating when he realized that Loki enjoyed the attention. There was a smile playing on his lips, which made him even more handsome for some reason.

As if Loki needed that.

The next time Samuel walked past Loki, the god leaned forward, clearly wanting Samuel's attention. Even though Samuel wanted nothing more than to run away, he stopped and focused on the god.

"How long have you worked here? Because I would have remembered you if I'd been since the last time I was here."

Samuel arched a brow. "Would you have, really?"

He hadn't meant to be rude, but he still realized how his tone could be taken. Thankfully, the god didn't seem to care, or maybe he didn't notice. He grinned at Samuel, his teeth very white in the half-darkness of the club.

"How could I have not? You're the most gorgeous person in the club tonight."

Samuel barely resisted the urge to roll his eyes. "That's bullshit."

Loki seemed delighted that instead of saying thank you, Samuel was contradicting against him. "Is it? Can you find one person who is more beautiful than you are?"

Samuel didn't have to look too far. He pointed at one of the men dancing. He was a regular, and he had everyone's attention when Loki wasn't there. He seemed a little miffed tonight, and he kept staring at Loki, but then, so did everyone else. "Him. He's beautiful."

And he was. Samuel didn't know his name, but he'd nicknamed him Blondie in his mind. The man was as blond as Samuel, but he was shorter. That didn't make him any less muscled, but his body was on the slimmer side, like Loki's. He was beautiful under the club lights, and he knew it.

"Meh," Loki said. "I mean, don't get me wrong, he *is* cute, but he's got nothing on you."

Samuel wasn't ugly. Many guys seemed to like the blond hair and blue eyes he had going on, which meant he never had to look for company when he wanted it. He wasn't quite sure if Loki was outright lying to him or if he meant it, but either way, why was he doing this?

Samuel shook his head. Whatever the reason behind Loki's words, Samuel was going to stay as far away from the god as he could. Loki had a reputation of getting everything and everyone he wanted and for not being picky when it came to getting people in his bed—or in the bathroom, or against the walls. Apparently, he wasn't picky about where he had sex, either. Samuel had heard many stories since he'd started working here, but he'd never become the protagonist of one of them.

He forced himself to smile anyway. He had to be polite and let Loki down nicely, although he wasn't sure that was possible. Would Loki get angry if he didn't give him what he wanted? So far, he seemed nice enough, but there was no way to know how a god would react when they weren't given what they wanted. The problem was that Samuel had no intention of getting involved with a god, even if it was for only one evening or half an hour. It would be too messy and complicated, and Samuel didn't do messy and complicated.

The problem was that Loki was staring at him as if he were a giant ice cream cone, and if there was a picture in the dictionary under the entries for messy and complicated, it had to be Loki's.

The bartender was barely looking at Loki, which wasn't what Loki was used to. Usually, the bartenders fell over themselves to give him what he wanted, and the other two people behind the counter tonight weren't any different. This one was, and Loki found he couldn't stay away.

He leaned over the counter, wanting to be closer. "What's your name?"

The man hesitated as if he didn't want to tell Loki his name. Maybe he didn't. He surprised Loki in a way that Loki didn't think any human could surprise him except for Jimmy.

Then the man looked at someone behind Loki, and he swallowed heavily. Loki turned around to find the owner of the club staring at them with his arms crossed over his chest, but before he could ask what was going on, the bartender finally answered his question.

"My name is Samuel."

"Can I call you Sam?"

Sam arched a brow. "Would you do so even if I told you no?"

Usually, Loki would have. He didn't care about what other people wanted, humans or gods. But for some reason, he didn't want to displease Sam. "Just tell me what you want me to call you, and that's what I'll call you."

Sam blinked as if he didn't understand what Loki was saying. "Sam is fine," he finally said with a grunt.

Loki beamed at him. "Good. I'm Loki."

"I'm pretty sure everyone here knows it. I certainly do."

"But we've never met before."

Sam looked at Loki as if he were stupid, which wasn't something that happened often. Most normal people, especially humans, were terrified that Loki would smite them. He had the power to do that, but he didn't usually kill without a good reason, and glaring at him wasn't one.

"Is there anyone here who doesn't know who you are, even people you've never met?" Sam asked.

It sounded like a rhetorical question, but Loki still felt the need to answer. "How am I supposed to know if people know me? I certainly don't know any of them."

"You're a god. You don't have to know any of them, but they have to know you."

"That doesn't seem right. No one *has* to know me."

Sam rolled his eyes. "Fine. They don't have to know you, but it's better for them if they do. They wouldn't want to disrespect a powerful god like you."

Loki couldn't stop smiling. He didn't usually enjoy banter with humans, but Sam was different. He wasn't fawning over Loki and rushing over to give him everything he wanted. If anything, he seemed annoyed by the attention Loki was giving him, which made Loki want to do it even more.

Sam wasn't the first human who acted as if Loki wasn't anything special, but he was one of the few who'd gotten Loki's attention. Usually, it was an act, but he could tell that in Sam's case, it wasn't. He didn't care who Loki was, and if Loki was reading him right, he wished Loki would stop talking to him. Loki suspected that if the club owner hadn't been staring at them, Sam would have told him to fuck off and gone back to work. Instead, he was forced to talk to Loki and give him what he wanted, and for the first time, Loki had a problem with it.

He frowned. He wanted to talk to Sam, but he didn't want Sam to feel forced to do so. Why didn't he want to talk to Loki, though? He might not be in awe of Loki the way most humans were, but he seemed to be especially opposed to having anything to do with him, which Loki didn't understand. It made him want to ask, poke and prod until Sam gave him the time of day and told him what was going on.

"Do you need anything?" Sam asked.

It was tempting to say that he did just to keep Sam here, but instead, Loki shook his head. "I'm fine, thank you."

"You said thank you."

"Well, I'm polite."

Sam snorted. "Somehow, I don't think this is normal behavior for you. But I have work to do, so unless you want anything else from me, I'll get back to it."

Loki waved for him to go. He stayed right where he was as Sam retreated. He couldn't look away from Sam, but he wondered what had grabbed his attention. Sam was different from Jimmy, and not just physically. Jimmy hadn't fallen all over himself to give Loki what he wanted, but he'd been in awe when they'd first met. That had quickly faded to friendship, and now Loki counted Jimmy as one of his closest friends.

On the other hand, Sam was clearly bothered by Loki's presence. Loki suspected that if Sam had things his way, he'd be kicked out of the club and ordered never to come back. No one would do that, and Sam didn't have a say in it, but it made Loki want to stick around even more. He liked doing what people didn't want him to do, after all, it was one of the reasons he was known as the god of mischief.

He grinned and took one last sip of his drink. Being a god of mischief wasn't a thing, but he couldn't deny he *was* a trickster. He didn't want to trick Sam, but he wanted Sam's focus on him much more than he should. He put the glass down, then hopped off the stool and headed toward the dance floor. He loved dancing, and tonight would be even better because he could feel Sam's gaze on him as he moved.

Loki placed himself in the middle of the dance floor, making sure to be in sight of the bar. He didn't look at Sam initially and instead focused on getting into the rhythm. After a moment, he almost forgot about everything and everyone around him and lost himself in the music.

When he was dancing, he didn't have to think about the people around him. He could feel hands on his body, some hesitant, some more sure as they touched him, but he didn't care. It was nothing out of the usual, and the people touching him didn't matter.

He did slap a hand that was headed toward his dick, and thankfully, he didn't have to do it again. Still, maybe ignoring the people dancing with him wasn't the best idea.

He opened his eyes, and his gaze collided with Sam's. Sam looked away quickly, but Loki had seen him now. He'd been staring, and the thought made Loki grin wickedly.

Even though Sam was trying hard to hide it, Loki had his attention.

Loki decided to experiment. He continued to dance, first mostly on his own, then with others. Every time he peered at Sam, the bartender was staring at him. He seemed torn, possibly between being jealous of the people dancing with Loki and not wanting to be jealous. Loki hadn't understood jealousy until recently, but now, he recognized it on Sam's face. It didn't matter that Sam quickly tried to wipe it away. Loki had seen it, and he knew Sam wanted him.

And he wanted Sam.

None of the people dancing around him were as good as Sam. Loki knew himself, and he realized that obsessing over one person, especially a human, could become problematic. That wasn't going to stop him, but it did make him slow down.

Even though he wanted nothing more than to head to the bar, grab Sam, and drag him toward the bathroom, he could tell Sam would tell him to fuck off if he did that. No, if Loki wanted Sam, he'd have to be smarter and much slower than he usually was. Normally, that would have annoyed him, but he found himself smiling.

Even though the bartender didn't know it yet, Sam would be his. Loki didn't know how long it would take, but it didn't matter. He was immortal, and he always got what he wanted.

Chapter Two

Loki wanted to scream. He almost did, but the people around him were doing enough of that, and it would be worthless to add his voice to theirs.

"I lost my son!" Frigg screeched.

"And surely you have to see how it was Hodr's fault." Odin sounded satisfied as he said that.

Frigg looked like she wanted to claw his eyes out of their sockets with her bare hands. "He's your son, too."

"He is no son of mine. He killed his brother."

"It wasn't his fault."

As one, they turned to Loki. He almost rolled his eyes, but he wasn't surprised they were trying to blame him for Baldur's death. They always tried to blame him for everything that happened in Asgard.

He glared at them and crossed his arms over his chest. "I wasn't even present when it happened."

"But the spear was yours, and it was made of mistletoe," Frigg snapped.

Loki raised his hands. "So? How was I supposed to know that Hodr was going to stab Baldur with it?"

"You knew mistletoe was the only thing that could kill Baldur. Why did you have a spear made of it?"

Loki could see where she was coming from, but he hadn't planned to have Baldur die. "It was a gift. What was I supposed to do, say no? Again, I never thought someone would use it to kill Baldur, least of all Hodr." Because Hodr was blind, and most of the time, he wouldn't have hit anything with a spear, let alone his brother — although often, family ties didn't mean much for deities.

It had been a freak accident. Loki hadn't been there, so he didn't know what happened in detail, but he'd heard several versions. What he did know was that Hodr had grabbed the spear while he and his brother had been playing around. Mistletoe was the only thing that could kill Baldur because of some prophecy or other, and of course, Hodr hadn't known the spear was made of that when he'd taken it.

He really should have stayed out of Loki's stuff.

But he hadn't, and after throwing who knew what at his brother without hurting him like they often did, he'd thrown the spear. Loki hadn't seen Baldur's body, but wherever Hodr had hit him, it had been deadly.

It didn't happen often. Most gods never died, even though it was possible to kill them. The only way to kill Baldur was using mistletoe, which was what Hodr had done.

And now, everything was a mess.

Frigg and Odin were blaming Loki for what happened to both their sons. No matter how many times Loki pointed out that he hadn't even been there, they wouldn't stop, and he understood. They needed to make the situation easier to grasp and accept, and having one child kill the other made it impossible. If they blamed Loki, they could overlook the fact that Hodr had been the one to take the spear and use it against his brother.

Loki had been trying to deal with the situation ever since it had happened several weeks earlier, but they were at a stalemate. Every time he came to Asgard, he ended in a screaming match with Odin and Frigg, and today wasn't any different.

He had a bad feeling about this. Gods had long memories, and they could hold a grudge. If Odin and Frigg truly believed he was responsible for their son's death, they'd get revenge. They didn't even have to do it now. The three of them were immortal, and they could wait until Loki forgot about this accident. He'd never see it coming, which was why he'd been attempting to make them see that it *was* an accident and that no one was at fault.

He pinched the bridge of his nose and decided to try again. "As I was saying, the spear was a gift. I kept it in my home, and I don't understand how it got out. Hodr might have taken it himself, which would explain how he didn't realize it was made from mistletoe. What I don't understand is *why* he went to my home to grab the spear."

Loki barely visited Asgard, including the palace he called home here. It was too big and empty, and he spent most of his time either in the human world or in Egypt. He disliked Asgard, and everyone here disliked him.

Odin jabbed a finger in his direction. "You're the trickster. You're behind all of this."

Unfortunately, the fact Odin believed that made sense. Loki did have a reputation, and this sounded like a prank he'd pull on Hodr and Baldur. Of course, if he'd knowingly given Hodr the mistletoe spear, it would have been more than a prank. It would have been murder, even though he wouldn't have been the one to wield the spear.

But he had nothing to do with this.

"Why would I have wanted to kill Baldur?"

"Because you're jealous or because it's part of one of your schemes. I don't know why you did it, but you'll pay for it," Odin spat out.

Loki crossed his arms over his chest and arched a brow. "Will I? What are you planning on doing?"

It was like poking a bear, but Odin knew how powerful Loki was. They both were, and if they fought, they'd both get hurt. Odin had been a fighter once, but now he enjoyed his cushy life in Asgard. He wouldn't want to do anything to put that in jeopardy, especially not fighting Loki.

Sometimes, it helped to have a reputation. Every single god in Loki's pantheon knew what they'd be up against if they went against him. No one wanted to do something stupid, not even Loki. The fact that they were stepbrothers—not father and son like everyone thought after those stupid movies— didn't change how they felt about each other. Odin despised Loki, and Loki thought Odin was an idiot.

"I lost two sons," Frigg lamented.

Loki was more than happy to turn his attention to her. "You only lost Baldur. You don't have to lose Hodr, but it will depend on the way you behave with him." Loki hadn't seen Hodr since before all this mess happened, but maybe he should. He doubted he'd killed his brother on purpose, and he was probably hurting over what had happened, especially considering his parents' reaction.

Odin puffed out his chest as if he were trying to intimidate Loki. "We will never forgive Hodr for what he did." Frigg looked like she wanted to protest, but Odin didn't give her the time. "He's lucky I haven't killed him."

"Why don't you?" Not that Loki wanted Hodr to be killed, especially considering the situation, but he was curious.

"Some people around here have forgotten who I am," Odin thundered. He stomped away, pacing the length of the throne room.

All around them were the seats that belonged to the Aesir, the most powerful gods in their pantheon. This was where they had their meetings, and Loki couldn't help but peek at his seat. He seldom used it, and he had no intention of coming around more often than he strictly had to. Still, seeing it re- minded him that even though Odin was considered their leader, Loki was just as powerful, no matter what Odin thought.

"We can't kill our son," Frigg said.

She'd always been a proud and strong woman, and that

hadn't changed, but the loss of her son had taken a toll on her. She was pale, and her eyes were red as if she'd been crying. She still tried to act brave and as if nothing had happened, but Loki suspected it was for Odin's benefit rather than because she truly felt that way.

"You're right," Odin said with a smile that made Loki shudder. "We can't kill our son."

Odin was planning something. Loki was torn between wanting to find out what it was and washing his hands of this entire situation. Whichever he decided, he doubted there was anything else he could do right now, so he stood up straighter and moved toward the entrance.

"Well, whatever happens, remember that Hodr is your son, too. Is the pain you're feeling over Baldur's loss truly worth losing another son?"

He didn't stick around to find out the answer to that question. He was pretty sure Odin would have tried to smite him if he had, but he wasn't looking forward to a fight. He had better things to do tonight, like going to the club and trying to woo Sam.

That would be enough to get his mind off what had happened, and he couldn't wait to finally be able to stop obsessing over it.

Sam knew the moment Loki walked into the club. He sighed heavily and looked up, and sure enough, the god was striding through the dance floor toward the bar. The people were parting like the Red Sea, and he didn't even seem to notice. His focus was on Sam, and while it made Sam want to squirm, he stayed right where he was and continued serving the customers.

If Loki wanted a drink, he could wait for his turn.

But he didn't have to. As soon as the customers noticed he

was there, they stepped aside, and he was able to make a bee-line for Sam. The woman sitting on the stool in front of Sam scrambled out of her seat so quickly that she almost fell on her face, but Loki didn't seem to care. He threw himself onto the stool and looked at Sam with a pout on his face. "I need a drink."

Sam had to resist the urge to scowl. His boss had scolded him the first time Loki had come, and he didn't want to go through that again. The guy had been clear that if Sam didn't treat Loki right, he wouldn't come back to work. Sam couldn't afford to lose his job, so he plastered a smile on his face.

"Do you have any preferences?" he asked.

"Oh, right, you're new. Cranberry juice, please."

Sam blinked. He waited for Loki to continue the description of the drink he wanted, but Loki wasn't talking anymore. He was staring at Sam, and Sam was staring back.

"Cranberry juice with what?" Sam finally asked.

"With nothing. I like cranberry juice."

Sam supposed that explained why they had several bottles in the fridge. He leaned down to grab one, but he didn't understand why Loki would drink cranberry juice. He'd imagined it would be something alcoholic that would get a human drunk with one glass, but Loki was only drinking cranberry juice. Why?

Sam poured it into a glass, added ice and a little umbrella, and slowly slid it over the counter. Loki grabbed it, downed half the glass in one go, lowered it, and sighed in pleasure.

Sam tried hard not to imagine what he would sound like in bed, but it was hard. The sight of his reddened lips did something to Sam's cock, and he was grateful the counter was between them so Loki wouldn't notice. He was the kind of person who'd tease Sam about it, and Sam didn't want that to happen.

"Can I get another one?" Loki asked.

Sam quickly refilled his glass, then turned to take care of other customers. After all, he wasn't Loki's personal bartender, and other people wanted to drink.

But no one else got cranberry juice.

Sam expected Loki to be gone when he turned back to him, but the god was still there. He was staring into his glass as if something heavy was on his mind, and Sam couldn't help but wonder what it might be. Loki was a god, and Sam had never really thought about what their lives were like. He didn't have to. Everyone talked about the most famous gods and what they did, including Loki.

Sam knew a lot about Loki, but none of that told him what had happened to him and why he looked so down. Should he do something?

No. He needed to stay away unless Loki called him over. He couldn't afford to be involved with a god, especially not one like Loki. He wouldn't mind getting a godly boyfriend like that pharaoh had, but the guy was a king. Sam was only a bartender.

The next time Sam walked past Loki, the god raised his glass, so Sam paused to fill it again. He was putting the bottle back into the fridge when Loki said, "Tell me about you. What made you want to be a bartender?"

The last thing Sam needed was to have a personal conversation with Loki, but he didn't have a choice. He was pretty sure his boss was keeping an eye on him to make sure he wasn't rude or something like that, but he supposed he could choose what information to share.

"Because it's something I can do."

"But surely, you can do other things? Why not be a dog sitter? Or an accountant?"

Against his better judgment, Sam found himself smiling. "Can you imagine me behind a desk the entire day? Or walking dogs?"

Loki stared at him for a moment as if seriously contemplating it. "I suppose I can imagine you with dogs. You look like the kind of person who enjoys being out in the open."

Sam shouldn't have been surprised that Loki could read that in him. The god was observant, which was why Sam was wary of having any kind of conversation with him. "I do," he confirmed.

"But you're not a dog sitter. You're a bartender."

Sam shrugged and raked a hand through his hair, pushing it away from his forehead. He needed a haircut, but he kept forgetting. "Why *not* a bartender?"

Loki frowned. "Well, I can think of several reasons. You have to work with crowds, which means it's noisy and smelly. You're on your feet all night, which can't feel good, and most people don't even say thank you when you give them their drink. I've also seen several fights start while I was here, and I wouldn't want you to end up in one."

Sam wanted to ask why not, but instead, he asked, "Have you ever seen *me* in a fight?"

"No. It doesn't mean it can't happen."

"Just like it doesn't mean I couldn't fall down the stairs or be in a car accident. I don't mind bartending. Sure, it's noisy, but I've always been more of a night owl, so it makes sense for me to work during the night. Besides, everyone here is nice, and my boss runs a tight ship. He doesn't want drugs around, and even though he closes an eye on the sex happening in the bathrooms, generally, people know not to do it." Except for Loki, but then, people tended to let him and all the gods do whatever they wanted.

Sam realized it had everything to do with the fact that a god could kill him with barely a glance, but it still pissed him off.

"What did you do before? Were you always a bartender?"

Sam didn't understand why Loki wanted all this personal

information, but beyond the annoyance it created in him, he didn't see a reason not to tell him. "I was. The bar where I worked closed, so I had to find something else. This one had an opening, so I applied."

"And now, you're here."

And some days, Sam wondered if it was a good idea, especially since he'd met Loki.

The god was interested in him. Even though Sam didn't understand why Loki felt that way, that much was obvious. He wasn't one of the people falling over themselves to give Loki what he wanted. Hell, he was barely polite.

But Loki had come back, and he wanted to talk to Sam. He was asking personal questions, which surely meant he wanted to know more about him.

Again, why?

"What about your family?" Loki suddenly asked.

"What about it?"

"Do you get along? Or are you always fighting?"

There was something there, and since Sam didn't want to talk about his family, he gently prodded. "Is that what's going on with you? Are you fighting with your family?"

Loki took a big gulp of his juice. "You could say that." He looked around, but no one was paying attention to them, which gave them a semblance of privacy. It was clearly enough for Loki, even though he leaned forward enough to not have to raise his voice over the music. "One of my . . . cousins? Well, no, I guess they're nephews. Well, one of my nephews, Baldur, couldn't be killed by anything except one kind of wood, mistletoe. He and his brother often had fun where Hodr hit him with whatever he could find. It was stupid, but it was none of my business, and I never played with them. I don't know what happened, but they were playing a few weeks ago, and Hodr found a spear that belongs to me."

Sam suspected he knew where this was going. "It was

made of mistletoe?"

Loki nodded curtly. "Yes. Hodr shouldn't have taken it. It was in my home in Asgard, and he should never have invaded my privacy, especially not to take one of my things. But he did, and he threw it at his brother."

"Is he dead?"

Loki grimaced. "Very much so. The problem is that Baldur's parents blame me for what happened. Well, they blame me, but his father blames Hodr, too. But I guess it's easier for them to blame me since I'm known as the trickster."

Sam didn't see how it could be Loki's fault. "I'm sorry for your loss."

Loki blinked up at him. "You know, you're the only one who said that to me. When I heard, I went to Asgard, but everyone's blaming me. They act as if I put the spear in Hodr's hand, but I didn't. I wasn't even in Asgard, and Hodr shouldn't have been in my house taking my things. I guess they all think I don't care about any of them or that Baldur is dead."

But it was evident to Sam that Loki did care. He wished he couldn't see that, because it made Loki more human, but he couldn't deny what was right in front of his face or the fact that he felt sorry for the god.

This was going to be a problem, but Sam didn't know how to stop it from happening.

Chapter Three

Once again, Sam knew the exact moment Loki walked into the club. It had become routine for both of them, and over the past few weeks, he'd gotten used to seeing the god and talking to him. He still wanted nothing to do with gods, but he couldn't deny he enjoyed talking to Loki. When the god wasn't maudlin, he was a lot of fun, and he'd lived through so much that Sam couldn't even imagine what it was like. Loki enjoyed talking about all of it, and to Sam's surprise, he enjoyed listening to the tales.

When Loki settled at the bar, Sam could tell something was wrong. He wasn't smiling, and he wasn't looking for Sam. Instead, he stared down at his hands as if they held the secret of the universe.

Sam exchanged a glance with one of the other bartenders. She shrugged and mouthed, "He's your regular." That meant she wouldn't step in to serve Loki and that Sam would have to do it. It was part of his job, but he didn't know how to deal with Loki when he was like this. He didn't think he'd ever seen it, and he couldn't help but wonder why Loki was even here. It was obvious he wasn't in the mood for anything the club could give, yet he'd parked his ass on one of the stools.

Sam dried his hands, hooked his towel at his waistband, and moved toward Loki. "Good evening," he said when he reached him.

Loki blinked up at him, but for a moment, it was as if he didn't recognize Sam. Then he smiled, but it was nothing like the smiles he usually reserved for Sam.

And yes, Sam knew Loki smiled in a certain way when he was with him and that he was the only one Loki smiled at like that.

"What's going on?" Sam asked when Loki didn't answer.

Loki shook his head. "I shouldn't have come. I'm no fun tonight."

Sam hesitated. He still didn't want to get involved, but he couldn't deny he'd started thinking of Loki as a friend over the past few weeks. For some reason, the god wanted to spend time with Sam, and he never pushed for something Sam wasn't willing to give. By now they'd had several conversations over a glass of cranberry juice, and while Loki had flirted, he'd never asked Sam to head to the bathroom or to see him outside of the club. Contrary to his expectations, Sam enjoyed the fact that Loki seemed to want to get to know him.

He enjoyed Loki's companionship, period.

But something was wrong with Loki, and since Sam considered him a friend, he wanted to do something about it. "Is it your family?" he asked.

The grimace on Loki's face was enough to tell him his family was involved. Loki hadn't talked much about them since the night he'd explained what had happened with his nephews, but Sam had looked them up. He'd recognized Baldur's name, although he hadn't realized he was Loki's nephew. Everyone thought Odin and Loki were father and son, but in reality, they were brothers. That meant that one of Odin's sons had killed his brother, and Loki had been pulled into the situation. The fact that people thought he was responsible for what happened was ridiculous, but Sam supposed he didn't understand gods.

Except that maybe he did understand one god. He'd gotten to know Loki, and he knew how torn Loki was over all of this. It would have been easy for him to wash his hands of the situation, but instead, from what he'd told Sam, he kept visiting

Asgard and trying to talk some sense into Odin and his wife.

Loki got to his feet. "I'll go," he said.

Surprising himself, Sam reached out and grabbed Loki's wrist.

Loki blinked at it, then looked up at Sam, and Sam let go. He waited for Loki to smite him because he'd touched him, but the god just stood there, waiting for whatever Sam wanted to say.

Sam wasn't sure. He hadn't been thinking, and now he tried to think quickly and give himself a reason for touching Loki. "Where will you go?"

Loki shrugged. "Wherever I want. Maybe Japan, although it's already morning there, and it doesn't fit my mood."

The fact that Loki could travel over the world with barely a thought was almost too big to wrap his mind around. Sam wanted to ask questions, but now wasn't the time. Loki was hurting, and Sam wanted to do something about it.

"What about your friends in Egypt?" Everyone knew Loki was close to the king and his entourage.

"I suppose I could go to them, but I don't want to bother them with this. I haven't told them what happened with my family. I haven't told anyone."

Anyone except Sam. Sam once again wanted to ask why, but instead, he made a rash decision that he hoped he wouldn't regret. "Why don't you sit again? I need to go see my boss, but I'll be right back."

"Why do you need to see your boss?"

"Because I want to leave."

Sam didn't allow Loki to ask any more questions. He tugged the towel at his waist free, dumped it on the counter, and walked around the bar. He knew where he'd find his boss, so he made a beeline for the office. After he'd realized that Sam wouldn't be rude and kick Loki out, Idris had relaxed and had stopped staring at them the entire evening.

Sure enough, he was behind his desk when Sam reached the office. He quickly knocked, then stepped in when his boss waved at him. "Is someone giving you trouble?" he asked.

"Not exactly, but I have a family emergency. I need to go."

Idris leaned back in his chair and stared at Sam for a moment. "Do you have an emergency, or does this have to do with a certain god?"

"I'm not running away from Loki, if that's what you're asking."

The corners of Idris's lips curled. "That *is* what I was asking. I know you don't like him, but you've been doing a good job with him."

Sam briefly wondered if Idris would be surprised to find out Sam was taking time off for Loki. Not that he cared, as long as he was allowed to take the evening off.

"Is he here right now?" Idris asked.

"He is, but I think he was leaving. He seems a bit out of sorts."

"Aren't they always? I suppose you can go. There wasn't much of a crowd tonight, and if the other two need help, I can step in for a bit. Will you let me know if everything is okay and if you need more time?"

Sam was surprised. Idris wasn't a bad boss, but he hadn't expected him to be so open to him taking time off. "I don't think it will be necessary, but I'll let you know," he promised.

"Go, then. Tell the others to let me know if they need help."

Sam didn't wait for him to change his mind. He turned around and rushed away, headed to the break room. He grabbed his jacket and backpack, then almost ran back to the club, wondering if Loki would still be there when he reached him.

He was. He was still sitting on his stool, and someone had poured him a cranberry juice. He wasn't drinking it, just staring into the glass as if he were trying to find answers to his problem there.

He probably was.

Sam walked behind him and gently touched his shoulder. Loki startled, then he relaxed when he saw it was Sam. "Let's go," Sam said.

Loki cocked his head. "What do you mean?"

"What I just said. Let's go."

"But you have work."

"Not tonight. I took some time off."

Loki gaped. "For me?"

Sam prayed he wouldn't regret this, but he nodded. "For you, and I have a plan."

Loki looked around. He'd imagined the place where Sam lived a few times, but this wasn't what he'd thought of.

"You need anything else?" Sam asked.

Loki shook his head and buried deeper into the blanket nest around his body.

He and Sam were on the roof of a tall building. They'd stopped in Sam's apartment to drop off Sam's jacket and backpack and to pick up blankets, food, and drinks. Then they'd hoofed it all the way to the roof. There was no elevator, and Loki had offered to use his powers to get them there, but Sam had waved him off. From the easy way he'd navigated the stairs, it was obvious he did this quite often, and Loki understood why.

There had been a few chairs by the door, but Sam had led the way to a battered couch. Someone had placed a gazebo over it, so even if it rained, it wouldn't get wet, and Sam had used the blankets to create a nest for them. He'd placed Loki right in the middle of it, had given him food and a bottle of water, and sat next to him. He hadn't asked Loki what was going on. He'd just been there for him, and Loki's mind spun with that knowledge.

No one had ever just been there for him except Jimmy. Everyone always had a reason they wanted to be around him, usually because they wanted to impress him, but not always. Often they wanted money and power, but Sam was different.

Loki peeked at the human, trying to read him but unable to do so. Usually, he had a good grasp of what was going on in humans' minds, but Sam was an unknown quantity. Loki didn't understand why he was taking care of him, and it made him feel a bit pathetic. Jimmy was his friend, so he wouldn't have minded, but why was Sam doing this?

"So, do you want to talk about it?" Sam asked.

He never looked at Loki—instead, he was staring at what they could see of the sky. He was clutching a bottle of water in his hands, and he looked at ease, although a bit tense.

The last thing Loki wanted was to talk about what was happening in Asgard, but he felt he owed it to Sam. He was being nice, and Loki should do the same.

Besides, he could trust Sam. They'd talked several times, because Loki was intrigued and had been going to the club more often, and even though Sam was grumpy and disliked the fact that Loki was a god, he was a good person. The fact that he'd brought Loki here was another example of his kindness, and he'd listen to what Loki had to say and would try to help him find a solution, even though it was none of his business and it would be better for him not to get involved.

It was never a good idea for a human to get involved with a god. It sometimes worked, like for Qebui and Jimmy and Sed and his king. But most of the time gods were a mess. They fought among each other and used every weakness they could to win. That meant using whatever human their enemy god loved, and unfortunately, Loki had many enemies. None of them would hesitate to hurt Sam if they found out it meant they'd hurt Loki, but that wasn't something Loki wanted to contemplate.

But he would have to. Odin was on the warpath, and he was aiming at Loki. For now, he hadn't done anything, but that would change eventually. Loki would have to deal with it then, and he didn't want Sam to get hurt, especially when he had nothing to do with the situation.

But Loki couldn't leave. Jimmy was busy, and while they were friends, he had Qebui to focus on. On the other hand, Sam was focused only on Loki, and that made Loki feel better. He could find someone else so Odin wouldn't hurt Sam, but they wouldn't be Sam. They wouldn't truly try to help, and instead, they'd use him. That wasn't something he wanted to deal with at the moment.

Loki sighed and tilted his head to stare at the sky, too. "You already know the situation up there. It's been getting out of hand, with Odin wanting to get revenge, even though Hodr is his son. I don't know what's going to happen, but it won't be good."

"What about Frigg? Doesn't she have a say in this? Both Baldur and Hodr are her sons, too."

"She's been trying to calm Odin down, but she's grieving. I don't think she's visited Hodr since Baldur died. No one has. They're afraid Odin will believe it means they're on his side, and I don't think they want to deal with his reaction." Loki had done many things over his immortal life, some bad, some not so bad, but he couldn't even begin to imagine how Hodr was feeling. He'd killed his brother, and even though it had been an accident, there was no way to get Baldur back.

Loki wanted to talk to Hodr, if anything, to ask how he'd gotten the spear, but Hodr had refused to see anyone, including him. He'd isolated himself, which might not be a bad idea, considering how angry Odin was.

He took a sip of water, even though he wasn't thirsty. It helped distract him from his thoughts.

"What do you think will happen?" Sam asked.

Loki shrugged. "There's no way to know. Gods are volatile on the best of days, and Odin is pissed. If I had to guess, I'd say someone is going to get hurt, probably Hodr."

"Does he have friends who can protect him? Or maybe you?"

"I'm trying, but he's making things harder because he refuses to see me. I've been attempting to find out exactly what happened, but no one is talking to me, and it's frustrating." It also meant he couldn't prove he'd had nothing to do with it.

No one cared that he hadn't been in Asgard that day. No one cared that he hadn't known Baldur was dead until several days after it happened. Frey had tried calling Loki, but he hadn't been able to get in touch.

It wouldn't have changed anything. Odin and Frigg insisted that Loki had a hand in this, and people were starting to believe them. Even though he hadn't been the one who killed Baldur, they couldn't believe he hadn't given Hodr the spear.

Loki didn't have a reason to kill his nephew. He especially didn't have a reason to make his death so cruel to everyone. And while he enjoyed playing tricks on people, he was never cruel. No one seemed to understand that, or maybe they didn't want to accept it. Maybe it was easier for them to continue convincing themselves that it was all his fault every time something happened. It meant they didn't have to take responsibility for what they did, which pissed Loki off, but what could he do about it? Even if he decided to stay in the human world and never go back to Asgard, they'd find a way to blame him for whatever happened.

"You're worried about your family, even though they aren't good to you," Sam said.

"I am. Hodr killed Baldur, but it was an accident, and I don't want him to pay for it with his life. I also don't want

Frigg to be overwhelmed by grief. I'm worried about both of them, especially because Odin will steamroll them. He always does."

"Because he is *the* god."

Loki snorted. "He likes to think he's the most powerful god, but that doesn't mean it's true."

"Who is then?"

"There's no way to know. We fight a lot with each other, but it's usually not deadly. What happened to Baldur is awful, but he's one of the few gods who died. We're immortal, even though we can be killed."

And the fact that Baldur could only be killed by mistletoe made all of this more horrifying. Loki should have been more careful with the spear, or maybe he should have destroyed it, but it had been a gift, and he hadn't wanted to be rude. Odin wouldn't understand that. Once Odin was convinced of something, he didn't change his mind, no matter what happened.

Sam wanted to do more for Loki, but he was afraid nothing he could do or say would help. At least Loki was more relaxed now, and he'd finally explained what was happening.

Sam wasn't surprised that gods were assholes. He'd thought Loki was one initially, too, and sometimes, he supposed Loki could be. But he'd come to realize that everything that people said about Loki and what they believed he'd done was just an image that Loki had cultivated, along with rumors and people wanting to badmouth him.

Loki wasn't human, but the emotions he felt were very much so. He clearly didn't know how to deal with them, but that was okay. Many humans didn't know how to deal with their emotions, either, but of course, they didn't have the power to kill someone with a flick of their finger.

But Loki wouldn't kill anyone. Sam had no doubt that he'd done so in his immortal life, and maybe he'd even killed people for no other reason than he could do it, but the Loki sitting next to him right now wouldn't do something like that. Sam had changed a lot since he'd been a teenager, and he could only imagine how much a god could change over hundreds and thousands of years. Maybe Loki had earned his reputation as a trickster and god of mischief once, but right now, he behaved like a normal human being who was having trouble with his family and didn't know what to do about it.

Sam had no idea what he was doing. He wanted Loki to trust him, and he didn't understand why. Why did he care whether or not Loki liked him? Why did he care about Loki's feelings in the first place?

"I'm sorry you have to deal with all of this," he said, still staring at the sky. It was an awkward position because of the gazebo, but the thing was useful when it rained. It kept the couch out of the elements, and it was a great place to sit during a storm, especially bundled in blankets.

But tonight was nice, too. The sky was clear, and Sam could see the stars. He suspected that he was enjoying the evening more because of the man sitting next to him than because of the stars, though.

He was touched that Loki had told him all of this, especially since he doubted Loki had told anyone else, except maybe his closest friend. Loki had told Sam about Jimmy, but he'd also mentioned he didn't want to burden Jimmy with all of this, so Sam couldn't be sure. As far as he knew, he was the only one aware of the situation, and it touched him in a way he didn't quite understand.

"There's not much I can do. We don't choose family, do we?" Loki said, gently knocking their shoulders together. "And I still don't know anything about yours."

He was trying to change the topic of their conversation,

and Sam didn't blame him. He'd want to talk about something different, too, if he were in Loki's position. Having to deal with all of this and thinking about it even when he wasn't had to be hell.

"There's not much to say," he explained. "I grew up in a normal family. My parents met in high school and got married once they were done with college. They had my sister, then me, then my brother. They raised us in your typical white picket fence house with a cat and a dog, and they still live there."

"That sounds incredible."

There was wistfulness in Loki's tone, and while Sam understood why, it made him uncomfortable. "I'd have called it boring, but sure. I suppose it *was* incredible. I never had to be afraid that my brother would kill me. They didn't even have anything bad to say about the fact that I'm gay."

"I never understood why some humans don't see that for what it is," Loki said, staring at the sky again.

"What do you mean?"

"Just that I don't get it. Most gods are pansexual, as you would call it. I suppose it has to do with the fact that we're immortal and we've had all the time in the world to explore our sexuality and have sex with as many people as we want. But many humans are stuck in what they think is normal, and they don't even realize it isn't. There's no normal. Everyone is different, but that doesn't make it a bad thing."

Sam knew Loki'd had both male and female lovers in the past. He even had a few children, but that wasn't something Sam wanted to think about, especially not the horse one.

That was just too fucking weird.

He cleared his throat. "Anyway, they don't live here. They're back in Minnesota, and I visit as often as I can. Between work and everything else, I don't see them much."

"So you're alone here?"

"Not alone. I live with my two best friends, Kimberly and Arlo. And of course, there's Misty."

"Who's Misty?" Loki seemed interested, but his gaze blazed with something Sam couldn't identify. He found himself breathless, and it took him a second to realize he wasn't answering Loki's question.

"My cat," he croaked.

Loki blinked, then laughed. "I like cats, and they usually like me. I didn't see her when we stopped by your apartment—though then I didn't see Kimberly and Arlo, either."

"They're both out, and Misty was probably hiding somewhere. She doesn't like strangers, but I'm sure you'll convince her to become your best friend."

"Why do you think that?"

"Because it's the type of person you are. When you want someone to like you, you do everything you can to make that happen."

"Do you think it's what I did with you?"

"Maybe in the beginning."

"So you think I tricked you."

"Not tricked me, just showed me what you thought I wanted to see."

"And what did you want to see?"

Sam didn't have an answer to that, so he shrugged. "I guess I expected you to be arrogant and nasty. You're not the only god who comes around the club, and most of them aren't as nice as you. You're nothing like I expected. You wouldn't be here with me right now if I didn't like you."

To Sam's surprise, Loki gave a little smile and pressed closer to his side. Sam didn't know what possessed him to do it, but he stretched out his arm and wrapped it around Loki's shoulders.

He was snuggling with a freaking *god*.

He turned his attention back to the sky so he wouldn't

freak out. "Do you know the constellations?"

"Who doesn't?" He pointed at the sky. "That's the Orion belt."

Sam had no idea which stars Loki was pointing at, but he didn't care. He nodded, and since he was paying attention, Loki continued.

"And that's Scorpius."

No one had ever pointed out constellations for Sam, and the fact that Loki was doing it made him feel special. Sam was worried that he was getting too close to the god, but he couldn't do anything to stop it. It was like watching a car accident. He knew it was about to happen, but no matter how many times he told himself he had to stop it, he wouldn't be fast enough. Loki had already buried himself into Sam's life and under his skin, and there was no digging him out.

Sam's eyelids grew heavy. He wasn't used to being home at this time of the night, but sleep was pulling him under anyway. He tried to resist and to pay attention to what Loki was saying, but he knew he'd lose the fight with sleep. He should probably say something to Loki so that the god would know what was happening, but he didn't want to interrupt him as he talked about the constellations and how much he loved them.

Sam had made Loki smile again. He'd made him forget about what was happening in Asgard, and that was all he'd wanted to do. He didn't want Loki to be sad, even though it was a ridiculous thought.

Eventually, Sam's eyelids closed. He was still aware of Loki's presence next to him for a while, but he wasn't sure when Loki stopped speaking. At one point, he felt Loki move, and he tried to wake up, but a gentle hand on his forehead and a voice told him to go back to sleep. He felt himself being picked up, and even though he usually would have freaked out, he knew he was safe.

No matter what Loki had done in the past, no matter what god he was, Sam felt safe with him.

Loki wasn't surprised that the day had caught up with Sam. The human was adorable when he slept, and Loki wanted to spend the entire night staring at him, but their chat about their families had made him realize he needed to put a stop to whatever was happening in Asgard. If he didn't, someone would get killed, and he didn't want to lose another god, even though he despised most of them.

He didn't cross paths with anyone as he went downstairs, and the apartment was as empty as it had been earlier. He'd followed Sam to his bedroom, so he knew where it was, and he made his way there. The only thing that had changed was the cat sitting on the edge of the mattress. She stared at Loki as he gently put Sam down on top of the bed and pulled a blanket over him.

Once that was done, Loki stopped in front of Misty. He held out his hand and waited for her to sniff it. He didn't know what she thought, but she didn't run away, which Loki hoped meant he'd been approved. He grinned when Misty butted her head against his fingertips, and he gave her a good scratch before stepping out of the bedroom.

Then he went to Asgard.

He preferred the human world to Asgard, even though he had a house there. All the gods did, and many of them spent their entire time here. They didn't mingle with humans, which Loki believed was one of the reasons they didn't change. They were never forced to think about what they did—their actions and behaviors. They continued living the same way day in and day out, decade after decade, fossilizing. That was what had happened to Odin, and Loki had sworn he wouldn't allow it to happen to him. He liked humans, and he liked seeing how different they were, both from gods and each other. He enjoyed spending time with many of them, especially Sam at the moment. He truly believed that was why he'd evolved over the decades and why Odin hadn't.

He walked into the palace where the Aesir throne room was located. He could hear the screams even before he reached the main room, and he sucked in a breath to steel himself against whatever he was about to walk into. He thought he recognized Frigg's voice, which wasn't surprising since she'd been screaming a lot these days.

This time, Odin and Frigg weren't alone in the room. Other gods stood around, watching them as they screamed at each other. Frey was there, so Loki made a beeline for him, knowing his friend would tell him what was going on. Frey was startled when Loki touched his elbow, and his eyes widened. He pushed Loki behind a thick column, obviously trying to hide him from the others.

"What are you doing here?" he asked.

"I thought I'd give this another try. What's going on?"

Frey shook his head. "It's Odin."

"It's always Odin. What did he do this time?"

"He slept with a giantess."

That surprisingly wasn't the most stupid thing Odin had ever done, and Loki wasn't surprised he'd done it, even though he'd just lost a son and Frigg was still grieving.

"But that's not the worst of it," Frey continued.

Loki groaned. "Of course it's not. Tell me."

"She got pregnant. The child was born this morning, and he's already grown."

So there was a new god in the pantheon. Well, Loki supposed he was a demigod, but he was Odin's son, which meant he'd be powerful.

"I won't let you hurt him!" Frigg screamed.

She threw herself at Odin, but thankfully, Frey's sister

Freya grabbed her and pulled her back. Frigg tried to claw at Odin's face, but it was a good thing she didn't manage. He wouldn't have hesitated to take revenge on her, even though she was his wife.

Loki decided it was the perfect moment to get everyone's attention. That way, Frigg would have time to calm down and realize that attacking Odin wasn't a good idea.

Loki stepped into Odin's path as he stomped toward Frigg. That stopped him, and he glared at Loki. Loki was holding his hands behind his back, and he gestured at Freya to take Frigg away. He hoped she understood and that she'd be able to.

"What are you doing here?" Odin snarled.

"I heard the screaming and thought I'd see what was going on. So, you cheated on your wife. *Again*," Loki added, to let Odin know what he thought about that. He might be a trickster, and he might be mischievous, but he wasn't a cheater.

Well, most of the time.

"All of this is your fault."

Loki rolled his eyes. "What did I do this time? Was I the one to impregnate the giantess?"

Savage joy deformed Odin's expression. "So you know."

"I know you had a son and that he's already an adult." Loki looked around. "Where is he?"

Odin gestured, and a tall, blond man stepped forward. He had to be around seven feet tall, which made sense, considering what his mother was. His features were all Odin, though, and the smiles on their faces were disturbingly similar.

"He was born to avenge Baldur," Odin declared, his voice loud in the room.

For a second, Loki didn't know what to say. That didn't last long, and even though he wanted nothing more than to punch Odin right on the nose, he kept his fists at his side. "How is he supposed to avenge Baldur? What happened to him was an accident."

"You tried to make it look like an accident, but we both know you were behind all of this. How Vali chooses to do this is his business. I created him, and he'll do the job."

"Hodr is your son, too. He didn't mean to kill his brother, and I can't believe you created another son to make him pay for that." Actually, Loki could.

That was the kind of thing Odin would do, no matter how stupid and awful it sounded. Loki was right when he'd said this was getting out of hand, and he wished he could have done something to stop it.

From the cruel expression on Vali's face, he didn't care that Hodr was his brother, even only by half. He'd do what he'd been created to do, which was to avenge Baldur's death.

The problem was, who would he take it out on?

Hodr was a given, and Loki hoped his nephew was safe in his house. As far as he knew, Hodr hadn't left since the accident, and he hadn't let anyone in. He should be safe there, but the problem was that Vali would turn his attention to someone else, and Loki had a pretty good idea who that someone would be. Odin had been telling everyone that Loki was behind this, and even if they didn't all believe him, Vali did.

What did he know, after all? He'd just been born, and he didn't know any of the gods watching him. He didn't know Loki, and if Odin ordered him to do something, he'd obey without thinking about it.

"You have to see this is madness," Loki tried.

"This is the only way to avenge Baldur," Odin spat out. "You should have thought twice before you killed my son."

"I didn't kill your son." Loki wanted to scream in frustration. "I had nothing to do with Baldur's death. I wasn't in Asgard, and the spear was in my house. No one should have removed it, and I still don't understand why Hodr had it. Have you asked him? Have you asked him what happened?"

"I don't need to know what happened. You gave him the

spear, and you guided him to kill his brother. This is all your fault, and you'll pay for it."

Loki was afraid that Odin was right. He'd tried to stop whatever was about to happen, but even though he was a powerful god, there might be nothing he could do about it.

Chapter Four

Loki was tempted to give up, but he couldn't. Especially with Vali in the picture now, someone was going to get hurt if he didn't find a solution. So he was still in Asgard, trying to talk to people and convince them that one, he didn't have anything to do with Baldur's death, and two, they needed to help him stop this insanity.

So far, only a few people were on his side, but even they were hesitant to stand up to Odin. Loki understood, and he didn't blame them for wanting to stay out of this, but he *did* blame them for refusing. They needed to take a stand, and they weren't.

He looked at the palace in front of him. He wanted to see Frigg, and he'd been told that Odin had left the house. Hopefully, he wouldn't come back anytime soon, and Loki would be able to convince Frigg that what happened had been an accident and that neither he nor Hodr should be punished for that. He'd tried seeing Hodr before coming here, but once again, the door had stayed closed, no matter how many times Loki pounded on it. Hodr wasn't helping himself by not talking to anyone, and while Loki understood why he wasn't, something needed to change, and soon.

He knocked on the door, more lightly than he had on Hodr's. It took a while for someone to open, but when a minor goddess did, she squeaked and closed the door again. Loki wasn't offended, and he waited, hoping Frigg would see him. He smiled when the door opened again, and the same goddess waved him inside.

She didn't look at him, almost as if she were afraid that if she did, she'd turn to stone. Loki wanted to point out he wasn't the Greek Medusa, but he didn't dare make fun of the situation. It meant a lot that Frigg had agreed to talk to him. He didn't want her to think he didn't take this seriously.

The goddess guided him to the inside garden. It was in the center of the house, completely private, and that was where Frigg was sitting. There was food in front of her on a table—strawberries, some pastries, and tea—but she wasn't eating. Instead, she was staring at her cup of tea, and Loki almost didn't want to interrupt her.

But he did. He cleared his throat, and Frigg jumped. Loki pressed a hand against his chest and lightly bowed at her in apology. She glared at him, but she also gestured at him to take a seat in front of her.

"I was sure Skadi was wrong when she said you were at the door. What are you doing here?"

"I was told Odin left a while ago."

Frigg's expression shifted so quickly that Loki almost couldn't identify the emotions there. She was angry, sad, and confused. "He did. He's with his *son*."

Loki grimaced. It couldn't be easy for Frigg to lose her son by his brother's hand, then, only a few weeks later, have her husband cheat on her to create another child to get revenge on one of hers. It was a complicated situation, but then gods never did anything simply.

"What are you doing here?" Frigg demanded to know.

"I wanted to check on you. I can only imagine how much you're hurting over what happened."

She stared at him for a moment, and he was relieved to see that she wasn't overcome with grief like she'd been the last few times he'd seen her. Hopefully, it meant he'd be able to reason with her.

"You said you had nothing to do with what happened,"

she said.

"I truly didn't. I can explain again if you want me to, and I hope that this time, you'll believe me."

Frigg nodded curtly, silently telling Loki to go ahead.

"Someone gifted me the spear. It was a long time ago, so long that I barely remember who it was. I certainly never used it, and it was in my house somewhere." Probably in a closet. He didn't spend a lot of time in his house in Asgard, and he wasn't the kind of person who liked to have weapons hanging on the walls. "I never gave it a second thought, and I wasn't in Asgard when Baldur died. I still don't know how Hodr got the spear and why he used it. I had nothing to do with it, and he won't talk to me."

"How can I believe you?"

Loki leaned forward. Frigg looked regal still, but it was obvious the situation was taking a toll on her. Her hair was slightly messy, and her eyes were red the way they always seemed to be lately. She was pale, and unless Loki was mistaken, she'd started biting her nails.

"Why would I do something like that? I realize I'm known as a trickster, and once, I was. I still am, in a way, but Asgard isn't my home anymore. I spend most of my time in the human world. I don't want to offend you, but I couldn't care less what happens in Asgard. But what I'm trying to say is that spending so much time in the human world changed me, and even though the old Loki might have done this, *I* would never have hurt you this way. Even if I had a reason to kill Baldur—and I didn't—I wouldn't have done it this way. What happened destroyed not only Baldur's life but also Hodr's, and I suspect, yours. I know you might never trust me, and that's fine, but please believe me when I say that I'm truly sorry for your loss and that I had nothing to do with it."

Frigg stared for a moment. Loki held his breath, releasing it only when she nodded again. "You're right when you say that you've changed," she said. "I would never have thought it possible, but I can see it. I'm glad you found something better in the human world." She looked in the distance. "Some days, I wish I could do the same."

"You can. You just have to leave this place and never look back."

Frigg's smile was sad. "But no matter what happened, Hodr is still my son. I can't abandon him, and we both know he's in danger. Do you know anything about Vali?"

"I only met him recently, just like you. I'm afraid you probably know more about him than I do."

"I don't. I didn't know of his existence until Odin told me about him." Her hands tightened around her cup so hard that Loki was afraid she would break it. "And I never want to see him again. I can't believe—" She pressed her free hand against her mouth for a second. "Well, I suppose I can believe that Odin did this. I don't understand why he's so angry at Hodr and why he won't admit this was an accident."

Loki didn't, either, but then he'd never understood Odin. The other god felt like he always needed to be strong, which explained why he was on a path for revenge. The problem this time was that one of his sons had killed the other, so if he wanted revenge, he'd have to take it against his own family.

"Would you talk to him?" Frigg asked.

Loki blinked. "Who do you want me to talk to?"

"Vali. I know that nothing either of us can say will change Odin's mind. I'll try, but I don't want to see Vali."

Loki doubted that talking to Vali would change anything, but he nodded anyway. "I'll go find him, and I'll ask him to take a step back."

After that, they didn't have much to say to each other, and Loki quickly left. He'd never been close to Odin and his wife, but he still hurt for her. He had children, too, and he could imagine how hard it could be to accept what had happened and how painful it was to lose two children that way.

Even though he didn't want to do it, he headed toward Vali's place. He'd had to ask around to find out where Vali lived, and he hadn't been surprised to find out it was one of the newer palaces built at the edge of Asgard. The palace looked more like a fortress than a home, which didn't bode well as far as he was concerned. No servant opened the door, either. His experience was very different from the one he just had with Frigg.

Vali opened the door himself. When he saw Loki there, he smirked and looked him up and down. Loki wasn't intimidated and was pretty sure he could take on Vali in a fight if he had to, but he hoped he wouldn't.

"What do you want?" Vali asked.

"To talk to you, and hopefully, to make you see this is madness."

"I don't need to talk to you. Nothing can change my mind, and I certainly won't listen to what an old god like you has to say about my brother's death."

Many gods would have been offended by Vali's use of *old*, but Loki wasn't. He *was* one of the oldest gods in this pantheon. "Hodr is your brother, too," he pointed out.

"Hodr is an assassin, and he'll pay for what he did, just like you will. It's why I was created, and nothing and no one will be able to stop me."

Vali stepped back and slammed the door in Loki's face. Loki stared at the hard surface for a moment before sighing. That hadn't gone well—not that he had expected it to. The problem was that he hadn't solved anything. Vali and Odin were still bent on getting revenge, and Loki didn't know how to stop them, or even if he could.

Sam was on his bed, scrolling on his phone while petting

Misty's head when Loki suddenly appeared. Sam jerked and yelled, sending Misty into a run. She dug her claws into Sam's chest as she did so, which made Sam wince, but as he was about to yell at Loki for doing that, he noticed Loki's expression.

Something had happened, and it wasn't good.

"What's wrong?" he asked, dumping his phone onto the nightstand and getting on his knees.

Loki opened his mouth, then shook his head. "I don't want to burden you."

"I'm asking you to. I thought we were friends?"

Loki narrowed his eyes as he stared at Sam. "*Are* we friends? Because I never wanted to be friends with you."

It would have hurt if Sam hadn't understood that Loki meant he'd always planned on being something more. He still wasn't sure what he thought about that, but he wanted to distract Loki from whatever had happened.

Sam could too easily imagine why Loki was distraught. As far as Sam knew, he'd spent the past few days in Asgard, but clearly nothing he'd said had worked. Sam could do nothing to help Loki in that situation, but here, in the human world, he could be there for him.

"I want to take you on a date," Loki declared.

Sam blinked, not having expected that. He knew Loki wanted to be with him as more than friends, but he'd expected a demand for sex, not a date. "Why?"

Loki looked at him like he was an idiot. "Because I want to woo you."

"Again, why? You can have any person in the world, male, female, or non-binary. Why are you so bent on sliding into *my* bed?"

"Do you think that's all I want? To be in your bed?"

Sam shrugged. "Possibly in the beginning. Now, I'm not sure, but I still don't understand why you want to date *me*."

Loki sat on the edge of the mattress and twisted around to face Sam. "Why wouldn't I want to date you?"

"Because you're not a dating god. Have you ever been in a long-term relationship?"

Loki scrunched his nose. "I don't remember. Probably."

Sam resisted the urge to smile. "Fine. Have you ever had a long-term relationship with a human?"

"The answer to that is no. It doesn't mean I can't have one."

"It doesn't. Why me?"

Loki pressed his hand on top of one of Sam's. "Why *not* you? You're beautiful, and, more importantly, you're my friend. You're gentle and caring, but also strong, and you won't take any shit from me. You don't hesitate to point out when I'm wrong, even though you know I could kill you with a thought. You're not afraid of me, and you don't want anything from me except myself."

Sam shouldn't have been surprised that Loki had been able to read all of that in him. It was true, too. He didn't want or expect anything from Loki, but he liked the guy, and even though he didn't want to, he cared about him. Loki wasn't just a god to Sam anymore. He was Loki, his friend, the man he was starting to fall in love with, no matter how terrifying that was. He was Loki, the guy Sam wanted a relationship with and wanted to take care of.

It was ridiculous to think that any god would need to be cared for, especially Loki. Sam could see it in his eyes, though.

But Sam wasn't an idiot. Even if he gave in to this, he doubted whatever was between them would last beyond the mess that was happening in Asgard. Loki was having trouble dealing with his family, and he needed support, which Sam was more than happy to provide. He'd be sad when things ended between them and Loki disappeared from his life, but as his friends had pointed out when he'd told them about all of this, he couldn't deal with a future he wasn't a hundred percent sure would happen. He had to focus on the present, and right now, Loki wanted to take him on a date.

"All right," he said.

Loki blinked. "All right?"

"You can take me on a date. I'm going to have to call off work, though." Sam could be in trouble if he did that more than once, but he had no doubt that Loki would intervene if he asked him to. Typically, Sam wouldn't do something like that, but if Loki wanted to take him on a date while he was supposed to be working, he'd have to take responsibility for it.

Loki bounced on the mattress. "Call your boss then. Take the night off, and please, put on some lighter clothes. The place I'm taking you is going to be very hot." He winked. "Just like you."

Sam opened his mouth to ask what Loki was planning, but the god had already disappeared. Sam wondered where he was for a moment, but then, a screech in the kitchen told him that Loki hadn't left the apartment.

Arlo could deal with him for the moment.

Thankfully, the call to Idris was quick. Sam explained that he needed to take the night off and that he was very sorry for waiting until the last moment to call, but Idris didn't seem to have a problem with it. He asked if a certain god was involved, and Sam couldn't lie to him. Idris was the one who'd wanted him to give Loki the time of day, after all. What was happening was kind of his fault, and Sam was thankful he realized it.

Once they hung up, he turned his attention to his dresser. He was curious about where the date would take place. When Loki had mentioned the weather being warm, Sam's mind had jumped to Egypt. Loki had friends there, so it would make sense, but would Loki want Sam to meet his friends already? Sam doubted it, so maybe it wouldn't be Egypt, but he still dressed with that country in mind.

Then he was ready. He headed toward the living room, laughing when he found Arlo and Loki on the couch, watching TV. Misty was between them, with Loki patting her head and Arlo patting her back. She was purring so loudly that Sam could hear her from where he was.

Arlo and Loki both looked at him when they heard him. Arlo grinned, but Loki was pouting.

"I'm much more handsome than the man who portrays me," he said, pointing a finger of his free hand at the TV.

Sam squinted, then realized that he and Arlo were watching one of those movies with the gods and many explosions. Arlo had no doubt started it on purpose, if the grin on his lips was anything to go by.

"I agree," Sam said, playing along.

Loki jumped to his feet. "I knew you would. Are you ready to go?"

Sam did a slow twirl so Loki could see him. "I think so, unless I need to change?" He was wearing a pair of shorts and a t-shirt, along with lightweight shoes.

"You're perfect," Loki purred.

Arlo made a strangled sound, but Sam ignored him. When Loki held out his hand, Sam took it.

He was surprised to find out that he trusted Loki completely, but maybe he shouldn't be. Loki had been burying himself into Sam's life since the first day they'd met, and now he was working his way into Sam's heart. Sam wanted to trust him, and he wanted to believe that Loki would never do anything to hurt him.

Only the future would show him whether or not he was right, and that future would only happen if he gave it a chance.

Which was precisely what he was doing by allowing Loki to take him wherever he was planning on having their date.

Loki relaxed as soon as he and Sam were in Egypt. It was so different from Asgard that it made it easier for him to forget about what was happening up there. The fact that Sam was with him also helped, and Loki was relieved Sam had agreed to come on a date with him.

He hadn't thought Sam would say yes. He knew Sam was still wary of getting involved with him, and he didn't blame him. Loki would be wary of getting involved with himself if he knew what was going on in his life, too. But Sam had known Loki needed him, and he'd said yes.

Loki didn't belong in Egypt. He had friends here, but he wasn't an Egyptian god. Still, both the people and the guards here had welcomed him more warmly than his family ever had. Odin was his brother, but they'd been at each other's throats since they were children. It hadn't changed over thousands of years, and Loki doubted it ever would.

He was close to a few gods in his pantheon but not as close as he was to Jimmy, Nu, and the others. If he had his way, he'd never go back to Asgard. He didn't feel like he belonged there anymore, but he also didn't feel like he belonged anywhere. Everywhere, he was an outsider, and he hoped that would change eventually.

"You weren't kidding when you said it would be hot," Sam said. He was pulling at his t-shirt repeatedly, trying to create some air. Loki almost told him it was useless. They were in Egypt, and it was hot as hell.

The problem was that he hadn't planned this date. He'd talked to Qebui a few times, so he had a few ideas about where to take Sam, but he hadn't thought it would happen today. He'd been impulsive, and now he wasn't sure what to do. Since his first instinct was to take Sam to the human palace, that was where he'd landed, and now he took Sam's hand

and led him through the gardens.

Sam was looking everywhere, his eyes wide as he took in the palace. "Where are we?"

"This is Mery's palace."

"You mean the king's?"

"Yes. We've become friends, and I don't call him king."

Sam snorted. "You're a god, so no one would expect you to call him king. Are we going to meet him? What should I call him? Your Highness or your Majesty?"

Loki laughed and pulled Sam closer, wrapping an arm around his shoulders even though it was too hot to do so. "Call him by his name. It's what he'll tell you, anyway."

"That's easy for you, but I'm just a normal kid from Minnesota. I don't know how to deal with kings."

Loki kissed Sam's temple. "You didn't know how to deal with gods, either, yet here we are."

Sam continued grumbling as they reached the palace. Thankfully, Mery had air conditioning installed, even though he tended to keep windows and doors open instead of using it. He didn't expect his guests and family to do the same, and Jimmy, who'd lived in North America for most of his life, kept his office cool. It probably wasn't the best place to start a date, but Loki needed help.

He stopped in the middle of the hallway, biting his lower lip. He could go to Jimmy, but what kind of signal would that send to Sam? He was already nervous about them being on a date. Meeting Loki's best friend would probably make him even more anxious, which was the last thing Loki wanted.

Instead of heading toward Jimmy's office, he pulled Sam the other way. Sam didn't say anything, and he kept staring at everything they walked past as if he'd never seen it. Loki supposed that was true. Loki was used to being at the palace now, and of course, he visited Asgard regularly, but for Sam, it was the first time he'd been in this kind of place. It made sense that he couldn't quite believe he was here.

They found their way to the kitchen. The people there were used to seeing Loki around, and they quickly bowed at him. He grinned, then gestured at the cook. "I need you to get some food ready for us."

"What did you need exactly?" the cook asked.

Loki wasn't sure what he and Sam would be doing, but a picnic didn't sound like a bad idea. "Things we can eat with our hands and that won't get us too dirty."

The cook quickly bowed. "I'll have that ready as soon as possible."

Once he was gone, Sam gently elbowed Loki in the stomach. "I don't think I've ever heard you sound more like a god than you just did. You ordered these people around, and they didn't even argue."

Loki frowned. "I should have said thank you. I'll make sure to do it when the cook comes back with the food."

"That's not what I was talking about. I was just teasing you, but it's obvious you're comfortable here."

Loki sat in a chair at one of the tables that ran along the wall, indicating for Sam to sit next to him. "That's because I am. I spend much more time here and in the palace of the Egyptian pantheon than I do in Asgard."

"Considering what I know about your family, I suppose it makes sense. What about a human home? If you don't stay in Asgard, where do you live?"

Loki waved his hand in the air. "Here and there. I have houses and apartments all over the world, and since traveling is so easy for me, I tend to spend every night in a different home."

Sam slowly nodded. Most people would have been impressed by what Loki had just said, but Sam didn't seem to be. Loki desperately wanted to impress him, but he didn't know how to do it. Usually he just had to flaunt his powers or how rich he was for people to fall at his feet. That wouldn't work with Sam, and it left Loki feeling lost.

"So you don't really have a home," Sam said.

"I have many of them. I just told you."

"No, you said you have many houses and apartments. I'm sure you own all of them, but does any feel like a home? Where do you go when you feel down and when you need comfort?"

"Here."

Sam cocked his head. "In Egypt?"

"That's where my best friend is."

"And your best friend is human."

"Jimmy, yes. He's from North America, like you."

"Am I meeting him tonight?"

"No. I doubt he'd want to be on our first date. Besides, I plan to have you by my side for many years. You'll have time to meet Jimmy."

Sam's lips curled into a smile. "You sound so sure that I want to stick around."

"Why wouldn't you want to?"

"I'm sure most people would fall all over themselves to be part of your life, but you know me better than that."

"I do, which is why I didn't try to buy you. I know that offering you money or power won't convince you to stay with me, so we're going on a date."

Sam stared at Loki for a while. He was still smiling, and he looked so beautiful in his white t-shirt that Loki wanted to kiss him. But the kitchen was no place for a first kiss—Loki immediately transported them to his favorite spot, the palace roof garden, where he set them down gently on a comfortable couch.

They were on a date. Surely Sam expected to be kissed? Loki wished to do so much more, but he didn't want to send Sam running. If they decided to do that, Sam would have to take the lead, and Loki would be more than happy to give it to him. This would be just a kiss, though. At least it would tell Loki how Sam might react if he tried anything else.

He leaned forward and smacked a kiss on Sam's lips. He kept it quick so he wouldn't freak Sam out, but when he leaned back, Sam hooked a hand behind his neck and pulled him closer. Loki was startled and squeaked, but he was more than happy to go along with the kiss.

Sam's lips were a little dry, but their gentleness more than made up for it. Sam didn't use any tongue, just pressed their lips together, but it was still the best kiss Loki ever had. He was slightly dazed when Sam leaned back, and he was grateful that Sam wasn't going anywhere. Instead of stepping away, he wrapped his arm around Loki's shoulders and pulled him close.

Loki complied. When he spent time with people, gods and humans alike, they expected him to take charge. They wanted him to be the protector since he was a powerful god, but Sam never had. He didn't see Loki as a god of mischief. He saw Loki as a man, and apparently, a man he wanted to kiss. That was something Loki had never had, and he'd do everything he could never to lose it.

Sam loved that Loki was doing this for him. He was a god, one of the most famous ones. He could have anyone he wanted with a flick of his finger, yet here he was, taking Sam on a romantic date as if he needed to try to get into his pants.

Sam couldn't deny he'd given Loki a bit of a hard time, but it wasn't because he didn't like the way he looked or because he didn't want to fuck him. He wasn't blind, and even more than being hot, Loki was nice. No matter who he was, he didn't look down at Sam, and that was refreshing. Many humans thought Sam was beneath them because he was a bartender instead of a lawyer or a doctor, but Sam enjoyed what he did most of the time.

Loki flicked his fingers, and the baskets of food instantly appeared. "Do you want one?" he asked, holding out a strawberry.

Sam nodded and reached for it, but Loki leaned closer and held it out to Sam's lips. Sam couldn't look away from him as he opened his mouth, and Loki slid the strawberry in. Sam bit down on it, and a dribble of juice escaped from the corner of his mouth and trickled down his chin. He felt like the heroine in a romance book when Loki leaned even closer and licked it off, and he'd have laughed at himself if he hadn't been so turned on.

Loki's lips moved from Sam's chin to his lips, and he grabbed Loki's waist to haul him into his lap.

Sam half expected Loki to protest and try to get out of it. Loki was powerful, and Sam was only human, so it would make sense if Loki wanted control in the bedroom — or in this case, on the garden roof of the palace. But Loki came willingly, and if the way he wrapped his legs around Sam's waist and settled in his lap was anything to go by, happily.

Sam tightened his arms around Loki. He was almost afraid to let go because he felt like Loki might vanish at any second. He could if he wanted to, and while Sam had initially wanted to stay away from the god, now, he couldn't imagine his life without Loki in it.

"No one will come up here," Loki murmured.

Sam opened his mouth to answer, but Loki thrust his tongue inside, and Sam could only kiss him back. He slid one of his hands under Loki's black t-shirt and felt the muscles of Loki's back shift and bunch under his touch. He knew what he wanted, but he didn't want to make mistakes that would push Loki away from him.

"You can fuck me," he whispered when Loki kissed down

his throat.

Loki nipped Sam's Adam's apple. "Is that what you want, or what you think you should want?"

He sounded amused, but Sam wasn't sure how to answer. Maybe he should trust the Loki he knew. So far, Loki had never threatened him. He'd never used his powers against him or against anyone else that Sam had seen. Sam had no doubt that he did and that he'd killed people in the past, but the Loki in his arms wasn't a bad person. He was used to getting what he wanted, and the fact that he was asking this made Sam wonder what that was.

"Sam?" Loki asked, leaning back.

Sam whined. He wanted Loki's lips back on his neck, dammit. "Yeah?" he croaked.

Loki was beautiful. He'd tied his hair back, probably because he was too warm in the Egyptian weather, and he was only wearing a t-shirt and a black pair of jeans. He'd taken his boots and socks off as soon as they'd reached the roof, and Sam had followed his lead.

They'd settled in the middle of a nest of pillows and cotton sheets, all of it spread on top of carpets. Above them was a gauzy gazebo that wouldn't stop the rain, but then Sam doubted it would rain. The thin material allowed them to see the stars, especially with the only other light being the candles lit around the nest. They were enough to illuminate their food so they could see what they were doing, and their light danced on Loki's skin, making him even more enticing. Sam wanted to touch, strip, and possess Loki, but he couldn't get the words to explain that out of his mouth.

Loki cupped Sam's face with both his hands. "What do you want? I know you were uncomfortable with me being a god, so if this is as far as you want to go, we can stop."

Sam had to clear his throat before he could speak. "I want more. I don't know what you want, though."

Loki's smile was a sight to behold. "Everything, but I know it's asking for a lot. We can start with good sex."

Sam barked out a laugh. "Sounds great. I, well, you can fuck me. I like it."

Loki cocked his head. "It doesn't sound like it."

"I do enjoy it." But it wasn't usually Sam's preference.

With the right guy, it could be great, and he had no doubt Loki would make sure he enjoyed everything they did, but his preference was the other way around. There was something about taking care of someone that way and becoming part of their body that hit Sam's button.

Loki sighed and kissed the corner of Sam's mouth. "But it's not what you want. I need you to be honest with me, Sam. If we're going to make this work, we both need to be." He paused and stared at Sam until he nodded. "Good. Then I want you to fuck me."

Sam blinked. He wasn't surprised that Loki was so blunt about it. Loki was blunt about everything. "You're sure?"

"Would I be telling you to fuck me if I weren't? I'm sure, and the fact that I'm a powerful god doesn't change the fact that I like being fucked." He huffed. "Humans have a strange view of sex. Why do you think that the guy being fucked is weak? It takes a lot to offer yourself to someone that way and to be able to let go of everything and enjoy it."

"I agree. It's just not something I expected to hear from you."

Loki snorted. "I think I've tried pretty much everything there is to try when it comes to sex. I know what I like and what I don't like, and I would love it if you would make love to me. There's lube somewhere in the blankets, although if you want, I can get myself ready." He winked. "I already worked on that when I showered before picking you up, so it won't be long."

The image those words created in Sam's mind made his

entire body flush. He wanted in to Loki's body, and he wanted it to happen now.

He grabbed Loki's hips and pushed himself up, twisting them around as he did so. Loki squeaked, but he didn't push Sam away, and when Sam looked at him, he didn't appear scared or indignant. If anything, he looked like he might tear Sam's clothes off if Sam didn't take them off himself, so he set to do just that.

It wasn't easy, because Loki kept trying to help him. They almost bumped their foreheads together at one point when they tried to kiss while Loki wrestled away his own t-shirt, but Sam jerked out of the way just in time. Loki laughed. The sound was bright and loud, and Sam dove forward to pluck it from Loki's lips. It turned into a moan as Sam pressed their naked chests together, and Loki grabbed Sam's shoulders and twisted them around again until he was sitting on Sam's thighs and looking down at him. He pressed Sam's shoulders against the sheets, silently telling him to stay, then got to his feet. He hovered over Sam as he slowly unbuttoned his jeans and slid them down his legs. Sam wasn't surprised to see that Loki wasn't wearing underwear, and he couldn't look away as Loki's cock appeared.

Loki was unashamed. He moved as if it didn't make any difference to him if he was naked or clothed, and once he'd thrown his jeans to the side, he crouched on top of Sam and helped him tug his shorts off. Sam was wearing underwear, but Loki made quick work of it, and it disappeared in the darkness over Loki's shoulder.

Sam wanted more time to stare at Loki's body, but Loki was on him again. He'd somehow already found the lube, and the snick of its cap opening was loud in the relative silence around them. Sam could do nothing but watch Loki as he reached behind himself. Loki was in charge, even though Sam was about to fuck him. Sam shouldn't have worried about any of this, and to be honest, he was relieved Loki had taken over. In time, he'd become more comfortable and would be able to forget what Loki was, but for now, this was better.

Loki's cheeks were flushed, and the tip of his tongue poked out of his lips. He looked almost like another person when thoughts of his family didn't burden him and when he didn't have to keep up an image for the rest of the world. Clearly with Sam, he could be who he wanted to be, and Sam liked that he could give him that.

Loki caught Sam's lower lip between his teeth and sucked. Apparently he was ready for more, because he wrapped his fingers around Sam's cock while pressing his other hand against Sam's shoulder. Sam anchored himself by grabbing Loki's hips, and he watched as Loki slowly lowered his body on top of his cock.

Inside, Loki was tight and warm. His body opened to welcome Sam. While Sam tried not to be too harsh, Loki had no problems. Like always, he took what he wanted, and he didn't stop until Sam was entirely inside of him. He'd let go of Sam's cock and had grasped Sam's shoulders with both his hands, but Sam unhooked them and twined their fingers together. Loki grinned at him and used that hold to push himself up.

Then he bounced down.

Sam gritted his teeth and let Loki do what he wanted with him. He felt he'd always want to do that, and for the first time, it was fine with him. Loki wasn't the man he'd expected — he was so much better, and Sam was falling for him. He trusted Loki, and he wanted to be what and who Loki needed.

Loki never hesitated, and his rhythm never faltered. He took what he wanted, and as he did so, he gave Sam what he needed. Maybe they did belong together, but Sam couldn't think about that right now. He could feel pleasure coiling in his groin, and when Loki tightened around him, he almost came. With a gasp, he untangled one of his hands from Loki's and grabbed Loki's cock. Loki keened and threw his head back as Sam jacked him off. His dick pulsed in Sam's hand, and Sam couldn't look away as it jerked and cum came out of it, splattering his chest as far up as his chin.

He'd done that. He'd made Loki come, and it had been incredible.

He didn't try to stop his own pleasure anymore. Loki had only paused for a moment. Now he moved again, sliding up and down Sam's cock. He had to be sensitive, but Sam couldn't have stopped him even if he'd wanted to. Loki's eyes had that gleam of stubbornness Sam could now recognize, and it didn't vanish until Sam cried out, clutched Loki's hands, and came inside him.

Sam's back bowed under the pleasure, making Loki squeak and hold harder onto him with his thighs. It felt like they were locked together, and Sam wished it could last forever.

Loki slumped on top of Sam, apparently not caring that he was smearing his cum over both of them. "So?" he asked.

"I'm not even sure I can speak."

Loki laughed. "You can, clearly."

Sam kissed the top of Loki's hair. "It was great."

"Of course, it was. I'm a god, and not only out of the sheets."

Sam's chest shook with laughter. This was Loki, too—he could make Sam laugh like no one ever had, and as Sam wrapped his arms around him, he prayed he'd never lose this. He wasn't immortal, but if he could have Loki in his arms for the rest of his life, he'd be happy.

Chapter Five

There was a bounce in Loki's step, and it was all thanks to Sam. He could hardly believe how happy he was, and to think it was all because of a human? *Incredible.* Most people in his life would never believe it, but he'd found his person, and he loved Sam. Whatever happened, Sam would never betray him, and he'd be there to help.

Of course, Sam wasn't a god. If something did happen with Odin, he wouldn't be able to do anything, but knowing he'd want to was enough for Loki. They were seeing each other regularly, and they'd settled into a kind of life Loki had never thought he'd have or want.

He'd never understood why other gods had relationships with humans. Most humans were boring, but Loki supposed it was because they tried to impress him. Sam never had, and not because he'd been trying to get Loki to see how different he was. He just *was* different, and he had no respect for Loki as a god or any other god. What was important to him was the kind of person they were, not their powers.

But for the first time, Loki wanted a relationship, and he didn't know what to do about it. Sam wasn't the first person important to him, but Loki wanted to do things the right way. Most of the others had been gods, and they'd understood him in ways Sam never would. It didn't matter to Loki, but he wanted to be sure he wouldn't make stupid mistakes that would drive Sam away from him.

Which was why he was standing in front of the door of Jimmy's office, ready to knock. The only reason he hadn't yet was the loud moan that had come from inside the room. Any other person would have quickly left, but instead, Loki grinned wickedly and pounded his fist on the door. "Qebui, let him go. He has work to do."

Someone in the office squealed, and something crashed to the floor. Loki snickered and leaned his shoulder against the doorframe so that when Qebui opened, he looked relaxed and bored.

Qebui glared at him. "What do you want?"

He was wearing the traditional white gown Loki had always seen him in and a golden necklace. His dark hair was all over the place, a sure sign that Jimmy had been holding onto it until a few seconds earlier.

Loki peeked around Qebui to find Jimmy sitting behind his desk. His cheeks were flushed and his lips reddened, making him look even more debauched than Qebui.

Loki snickered. "A little bit of afternoon delight?"

Qebui's glare deepened, but thankfully, he stepped aside to let Loki in instead of telling him to fuck off. It wouldn't be the first time they'd bickered over Jimmy, and Qebui still smarted over the fact that Loki had taken Jimmy on a date to Paris.

"You know, I wouldn't have taken Jimmy on that date if you'd taken your head out of your ass faster," he pointed out as he walked in.

Jimmy groaned. "Can we please not talk about that anymore? It's over and done with. The date was great, but it was nothing like our first date, Qebui. Besides, I've never been in love with Loki, but I love you."

Before, Loki would have been jealous of Jimmy and Qebui's relationship, but now he could imagine himself and Sam saying the same things and teasing each other. It made him smile, and it grabbed Jimmy's attention.

"All right, what's up with you?" he asked. "I can see

something is turning in your mind, and I'm curious."

They knew about Sam because Loki had asked Qebui where to take him for dates, but they hadn't met him yet, and they didn't have any details. Loki felt the need to keep Sam to himself for a bit longer, although he wouldn't be able to do that forever. Besides, he wanted Sam to meet his friends, and he wanted them to get along. Sam belonged in his life now, just like Jimmy and Qebui did.

He settled into one of the chairs in front of Jimmy's desk and put his boots on the desk. Jimmy glared, which caused Loki to snicker again and lower his feet to the floor. "I wanted some advice," he said.

Jimmy leaned forward. "About what? The human you've been hiding?"

"I haven't been hiding Sam. We even came here on a date recently."

"I know. The cook told us what he prepared for you. I was starting to think that Sam didn't even exist, so imagine my surprise to find out he'd been around and you hadn't introduced him to me."

Loki wiggled his eyebrows. "We were a bit busy, but I promise I'll introduce the two of you soon."

Qebui groaned and buried his face in his hands. "Please. I don't want to hear what you and your boyfriend are up to."

"So he *is* your boyfriend?" Jimmy asked before Loki could answer.

"He is," Loki confirmed, feeling like his heart might burst. "We've been seeing each other almost every day, and I spend the night at his apartment when I can." Which, too, was almost every day. Loki didn't want to waste one second away from Sam, and since he doubted there was anything he could do for the situation in Asgard, he hadn't gone back yet.

He was worried, but with no one listening to him and Hodr not talking, what could he do? He couldn't attack Odin and

Vali because they hadn't done anything yet. If he did, he'd be in the wrong, and they'd use that against him.

"That does sound serious," Jimmy said. The smile on his face told Loki he wasn't done teasing. "When's the wedding, then? And are you planning on having children?"

"Parenthood isn't that bad," Loki pointed out.

"That's right. I always forget you have children." Jimmy grimaced. "No offense, but I'd rather not think about the horse one."

Loki loved Sleipnir as much as his other children, but he couldn't deny that hadn't been his most brilliant idea. Nothing about that mess had been brilliant. "Sam doesn't want to talk about him, either."

"I think that's understandable, considering he's human. You know, before we meet you gods, we know about you and the stories, but it doesn't feel real. I mean, you guys are in the movies and everything."

"I've never been in a movie," Qebui grumbled.

Loki raised his chin high. "That's because you're not as handsome as I am."

Qebui snorted. "Or maybe it's because I'm a minor god. I don't want to be in a movie anyway. Have you seen the actor they chose to portray you?"

"What do you need from me?" Jimmy asked, raising his voice.

Clearly Jimmy knew where the conversation was going, so it was a good idea to stop it before it happened. When Loki got started on that actor, he never stopped talking.

Loki sighed. "I don't know. I guess I'm afraid of messing things up. Sam is important to me, but I don't do relationships."

"You were ready to do relationships for me, though."

"And I'll do what I can to make Sam happy, but everything is so complicated except what's between us. What if, in the end, he doesn't like the fact that I'm a god?"

"I don't think he cares that you're a god. I certainly don't care that Qebui is one. The only thing I care about is that Qebui is Qebui, and that's what I love about him. I'm sure the same will go for Sam."

"What if I'm not good enough?"

Jimmy's smile was gentle, and he leaned forward to pat Loki's hand. "You're a great person. I'm not the only one to think that. I know many people don't trust you and even dislike you, but it's because you've never shown them the real Loki. You're not hiding from Sam, though. He knows who you are, and that would mean a lot to him. Continue doing so and be honest with him. Right now, at the beginning of your relationship, that's all he needs."

Loki hoped Jimmy was right. Jimmy knew much more about being human and dating one than Loki ever would, so he'd follow his advice and pray for the best.

"So, you're in a relationship," Arlo said.

Sam wasn't sure how to answer that. He felt he and Loki were dating, but they hadn't talked about it. Loki had been saying he wanted to woo Sam, and he certainly had, but did that mean they were in a relationship?

"I don't know if I would call it a relationship," he said so he wouldn't expose himself too much.

Kimberly snorted. "What would you call it? He took you on a date to Egypt. He's been spending every night with you in your room, and trust me, Arlo and I both know what you've been up to in there." She leaned forward on the armchair she was curled into, almost dropping her glass of wine on the floor. "Does he have a brother?"

Sam grimaced at the thought of Odin. "He does, but I hope you'll never meet him."

Kimberly leaned back. "That bad, huh?"

"Pretty much. Loki's been having trouble with his family, and I kind of hate them for it."

"So you care about him," Arlo said.

Sam hesitated. He did care about Loki, but he suspected the relationship wouldn't last long once the problem with his nephews had been resolved. He wanted it to, but would Loki?

Sam wasn't stupid. He was only human, and he wasn't that exciting. Aside from Loki, his life was pretty boring. He shared an apartment with two people, had a cat, and worked at the bar. That was pretty much it, and considering Loki's life, how could it be enough for him?

But Sam wanted to believe it would be, at least for a while. Loki was immortal, so Sam's life would be like a second to him. Maybe they could be together until Sam died?

But Sam didn't want to think about that. It wasn't his own death that terrified him, but the thought of Loki losing him. If Loki was in love with him the way he was in love with Loki, it was horrifying to think he'd have to go through that and that he probably already had. He'd said he didn't have many relationships and that the few he did have had been with gods, and that was understandable. It might also be one of the reasons he could decide to break up with Sam. Who would want to be with someone when they knew they'd have to watch them die?

Arlo poked at Sam's thigh with his foot. "Sam?"

He forced himself to smile, but he suspected he didn't do a great job of it from Arlo's frown. He was sitting on the other side of the sofa, opposite Sam, their legs tangled together at the center since they were both sideways.

"You can talk to us," Kimberly murmured.

"We're a bit worried about you," Arlo continued. "I mean, we're glad you found someone you want to be with, but I'll admit I was stunned when I realized who he was. You've never made it a secret that you dislike gods, yet you're in a relationship with one." He hesitated. "He's not forcing you, is he?"

The thought was ridiculous, but Sam might have thought the same thing before he'd gotten to know Loki. "He's not forcing me to do anything. He's not that kind of person."

"He's a god. You always say they do what they want and that they don't care about consequences."

Sam sighed and tilted his head back against the couch to stare at the ceiling. "Loki isn't like that. I thought he was, in the beginning, but he doesn't act like most gods. He's just a guy, you know?"

"A guy who can take you on dates to Egypt," Kimberly pointed out.

"But that's not what I like about him."

"What do you like about him?"

Sam took a moment to gather his thoughts so he could answer truthfully. "He's powerful, possibly one of the most powerful gods I've ever met, but he acts as if he's one of us. He interacts with humans as if they're his equals, and he truly believes they are. I think that even though he has more power, he just sees us as being different from him, not lower. And yes, his powers allow him to take me on dates around the world, but what I like best is when we're in bed here together. We cuddle and talk, and he asks so many questions about the human world and the humans who live in it. He's curious, and he realizes he doesn't know everything, even though he's a god. And he cares about his family. He might act as if he doesn't and like they're nothing more than an annoyance, but that's not true. He even cares about the gods who want to see him dead or who dislike him for no reason."

"But he comes with many problems," Arlo said. His expression was serious as he stared at Sam.

"He does, which is one of the reasons I've been wondering

if I should be in a relationship with him. I might have chosen not to be if I hadn't seen how much he cares, but the reason he's involved in this mess happening in Asgard is that he does. Can I really break up with him because he cares too much?"

"You can if it's the best for you."

It probably would be, but Sam didn't want to break up with Loki. Being with him was a recipe for a disaster, and Sam might be forced to be involved in that disaster eventually, but Loki was smart, funny, and fascinating. He was like no one Sam ever met, and Sam had never felt the way he did for anyone else. Would he be able to find the same kind of love if he broke up with Loki?

"I think I'll see where things go," he said. "If they become too much for me to deal with, or if they become dangerous, I suppose I could break up with him."

Arlo poked him again. "But you won't." He took a sip of his wine while staring at Sam.

"I've never felt this way with anyone else before. I don't want to break up with him. I don't want to lose him. It doesn't have anything to do with the fact that he's a god and everything to do with the kind of person he is. Many people think badly of him because of rumors and things he did in the past, and they treat him in a way he shouldn't be treated. Most humans only want power and money from him, while most of his family hates him and wishes they could kill him. He has friends, but he's been keeping a distance with them because he doesn't want to involve them."

"But he wants to involve you," Arlo pointed out.

"Not really. He's been telling me about what's going on with his family, but it's not like he's taken me to Asgard, and I doubt he's told anyone up there that he's with me. Most of them would be stunned to find out he's with a human, so I doubt they'll even realize we're together if they meet me."

"It could be dangerous."

"But it could also be incredible," Kimberly intervened. "It's the first time I've heard Sam talk about a guy this way. He's really into Loki, and he shouldn't have to take a step back because of Loki's family. It's not fair."

"What won't be fair is if Sam gets hurt because of it," Arlo snapped out.

Kimberly scowled at him. "Who said he was going to get hurt? He's clearly in love with Loki, and I'm pretty sure Loki is in love with him. He'll do anything he can to protect Sam. Besides, something could happen to Sam even if he was in a relationship with a human."

"No human can throw thunderbolts."

Sam didn't want his best friends to fight. "That's Zeus," he said.

Arlo moved his glare from Kimberly to Sam. "Does it matter? You know what I meant."

"I also know that like Kimberly said, Loki won't let anyone hurt me. I'm more worried about him getting hurt."

"And you don't care if he keeps your relationship from his family?"

"I'd be relieved if he did. He doesn't trust any of them, which means I don't trust them, either. I also have no intention of ever going to a family dinner, so honestly, it's better if they never know about me. The people who are important to Loki do, and that's all that matters."

"Just be careful," Arlo begged.

"You know me. I'm always careful."

Except that in this situation, he hadn't been careful with his heart, and now it belonged to Loki. There was only one way to know whether or not it would be a disaster, and that was to see what would happen next.

Chapter Six

Loki wasn't feeling great, but he'd never let that ruin his date with Sam. As a god, he couldn't get sick, but he wouldn't be surprised if someone had tried to poison him. Vali hadn't done anything yet, but Loki was convinced he'd strike soon, and poisoning him might be the best way to get him out of the situation quickly and efficiently. Of course, Vali would have had to have found a poison that worked on gods, but Loki wouldn't put it past him.

He shook his head. He hadn't been poisoned, and he needed to stop worrying about that. He'd probably eaten something weird. He'd been taking Sam on dates around the world, and Sam had been enthusiastic about tasting local food. Maybe one of those disagreed with Loki's stomach, but he was sure he'd be fine again soon. It did remind him of something, a sensation he'd already lived through in the past, but his life had been so long that he couldn't quite pinpoint it.

So, instead of continuing to try, he wrapped his arm around Sam's shoulders and pulled him close.

The date was a bit cheesy, but Sam seemed to enjoy Venice. They were on a gondola right now, being taken down the canals. The weather was a bit cool, but Loki had thought of that and had brought a blanket. It was draped over both their laps. He never wanted Sam to be uncomfortable, cold, or hungry, not when there was something he could do about it.

Sam snuggled against Loki's side. "This is incredible," he murmured.

"I thought you didn't like when I popped you around the

world like this."

"I didn't in the beginning. I thought you were showing off, and okay, I was a bit jealous. I've always wanted to visit Venice."

"Are there any other places you've always wanted to visit?"

Sam looked up at Loki. "What will you do if I say yes?"

"I'll take you there, of course."

Thankfully, Sam wasn't annoyed by the show of power. He grinned and pushed closer, kissing the side of Loki's jaw. "Maybe I'll let you know then. I have to admit this is a handy power to have."

It was. Loki could be in Egypt with his best friend one moment and with Sam the next. Then, yet another moment, he could take Sam on dates in Venice. What more could he want? He had the man he was falling in love with by his side, and Sam was smiling at him so sweetly.

Loki leaned down to kiss him, but his phone vibrated in his pocket before their lips could touch.

He grunted and leaned his head back. "I'll ignore it."

"Don't. What if it's your family?"

"I'm sure they can deal with whatever mess they've made now." But Loki slid his phone out of his pants, thankful to see it was Frey until he realized that Frey would only call him for one reason.

Loki's stomach dropped, making his nausea even worse. "I think something happened," he whispered.

Sam sat up. "Answer, then. If something *has* happened, you need to know what it is."

Loki didn't want to find out. He'd pretty much washed his hands of whatever Odin was doing, but he'd known something would break eventually. He didn't want to be involved anymore, and he didn't want his date with Sam to be ruined.

Sam seemed to be able to read his mind because he kissed

his cheek. "We can have other dates in Venice," he murmured.

"I don't want your day to be ruined."

"Would you think your day was ruined if I got a phone call from my mother because something happened to my father?"

"Of course not. I'd get you there in seconds without asking about it."

"I can't do that for you, but I think you should answer that call."

"My family isn't like yours."

"I know, but they're still family, and you worry about them."

Loki did, so, with one last sight, he answered the phone.

"Finally," Frey snapped.

"You caught me in a bad moment. I'm on a date, so be quick."

There was a moment of silence before Frey answered. "On a date?"

"Did you call to find out who I'm on this date with? Or do you have something to tell me?" Loki was pissed, and he realized he shouldn't be taking it out on Frey, but he couldn't help it.

"You'll answer my questions about that later." His tone grew more serious. "Hodr is dead."

Loki briefly closed his eyes. "What happened?"

"Vali. He did what he'd said he'd do, and he killed him."

"And I couldn't stop it."

"How could you have? Hodr wouldn't talk to you or anyone else, not even his mother."

"How did you find out?"

"She went to try to talk to him again and found the door open. She went inside and found him. The, um, the screams alerted us that something had happened."

Loki swore. Odin and Vali were idiots, but they were

dangerous idiots. They'd taken Hodr's life, even though there'd been no reason to. Loki didn't care what they said about revenge. What had happened had been an accident, and Hodr hadn't deserved this.

"How is Frigg?"

"How do you think she is? She alternates between crying and wanting to kill both of them with her bare hands. Freya and I have been keeping an eye on her, but eventually she'll take things into her own hands. It won't end well, Loki."

"All right. Give me a few moments, and I'll join you."

"We're at my house."

That was all Loki needed to know. He hung up, sucked in a breath, and turned to look at Sam.

Sam didn't even give him the time to speak. "Go. They need you."

"They do. Hodr is dead."

Sam grimaced. "I imagined something like that happened when I heard your side of the conversation. I'm sorry you lost him."

"We weren't close, but he was still my nephew, and I feel responsible."

Sam took Loki's hand. "Because of the spear?"

"It was mine, and I still don't know how he got it." The more Loki thought about it, the stranger it was to him that Hodr had walked into his house when he never had before, poked around, and found the spear, of all things. What were the odds? There was something weird happening there, and Loki would probably never find out now that Hodr was dead. He should have insisted on talking to him when he'd still been able to, dammit.

"You'll find out." Sam's trust in Loki was humbling, and Loki hoped he was right.

If someone else was involved and had set up Hodr to kill his brother, they needed to pay for it. Only one person would be able to find out what had really happened because only one person cared about the truth—Loki. Frigg was grieving for two sons now, while Odin was a stubborn asshole who'd killed his own son, even though he hadn't done it himself. Who else would try to find the truth?

Loki kissed Sam's forehead. "Ready to go?" He'd already paid the gondola owner, so there was nothing that kept them here.

Sam nodded. "Take me home, and please, let me know what happened when you can."

"It'll probably be a while."

"That's fine. As long as you're safe, I can wait."

Loki took them to Sam's apartment, but it was hard to leave Sam behind. Sam had gone to work regularly since they'd started dating, but Loki had gone to the club, so they'd been together even then. It was a lot, but Loki couldn't stay away from Sam. Now he'd have to, and he was afraid something might happen to Sam if he wasn't with him.

Sam obviously noticed his hesitancy because he said, "I could come with you."

Loki's first instinct was to say no. He didn't trust his family around Sam. So far, only the people he trusted with his life knew about him, and Loki wanted to keep things that way, but he knew he wouldn't be able to. Eventually, someone would find out about Sam, so maybe it would be better to be upfront about who he was and what Loki would do to anyone who dared even think about hurting him.

This was a situation Loki had never had to deal with, and he didn't know what to do.

Sam didn't want to do it. The last thing he wanted was to deal with Loki's family, but he could tell Loki didn't want to face this alone. Who would? Over just a few weeks, Loki had lost two nephews, and he was still being blamed for the death of the first one. He'd known something would happen, but he hadn't been able to stop it and save his other nephew.

Sam didn't understand how most gods thought. He couldn't wrap his mind around the fact that Odin had created another son just to kill the one he already had, but then he was relieved he didn't understand. He didn't want to think like a god. He didn't want anything to do with any gods except Loki.

But Loki needed him.

Being in a relationship meant compromises, and so far, Loki had been the only one to do so. He'd fit seamlessly in Sam's life, but Sam hadn't made much of an effort to fit into Loki's. Yes, he'd met his friends, and they were the people who mattered the most to him, but he hadn't been able to do anything to support Loki during this situation. Now, he could go with him to Asgard and support him once he was there.

He realized it might make Loki more vulnerable. Loki would do anything to protect Sam, and with so many gods altogether and heightened emotions, there was a definite possibility that one of them would snap. Sam didn't want anyone to get hurt, least of all Loki, but he also wanted Loki to know that if he wanted, he'd come along.

Loki stared at him for a moment. "You'd do that for me?"

"I'd do this and much more for you." It was a gamble to put himself out there, but Sam trusted Loki with his heart.

Loki took one of Sam's hands and squeezed. "But you hate gods."

"I'm not looking forward to meeting any of them, especially after what you've told me about them, but I'd be doing this for you, not for them. And I like you, even though you're a god."

"I don't want you to regret it. I can deal with this on my own. I have before."

"That doesn't mean you should have to do it on your own, especially now that we're together. I want to support you and be there for you."

"As long as you're sure, I would love to have you with me. Maybe you'll be able to talk some sense into those idiots."

Sam snorted. "I can't even talk sense into you, so I doubt it, but if you want me to try, I will." Sam hesitated. "Will I be safe if I come?"

Loki's expression turned fierce. "They'll have to walk over my dead body if they want to get to you."

"Yeah, well, I don't want you to die."

Loki laughed and wrapped an arm around Sam's shoulders, pulling him close. "I won't die. Only a few gods could kill me, and even they would find it difficult. But if you're really worried, I want you to call Qebui if anything happens. He'll help you."

"Even if he has to come to Asgard to do it? He's an Egyptian god, and he doesn't belong there."

"Just like I don't belong in their palace, yet I visit often. I'll have to introduce you to Nu sometime. They're one of the oldest gods in the Egyptian pantheon, and they're awesome. I consider them a close friend, and they'll come, too, if you need them."

Sam hoped his presence in Asgard wouldn't create a war between pantheons, but honestly, he didn't care much. He only cared about Loki and being there for him. "Let's go, then."

Loki didn't ask Sam if he was sure. Sam was grateful for that, because he was afraid he'd change his mind and because it showed that Loki knew him. Once he made a decision, he tried to stick with it, and today wasn't any different.

Sam closed his eyes, then quickly reopened them. It didn't take more than a few seconds for Loki to move them around the world, and he expected the same to happen when it came to Asgard. Sure enough, they weren't standing in his apartment anymore. Instead, they were in front of a palace.

It sprawled in front of Sam, all white stone and stark angles. Sam didn't have the time to ask who it belonged to. They'd appeared right in the middle of a fight, or what looked like it might become one if someone didn't intervene.

A tall man stood in front of the palace with his arms crossed over his chest. His blond hair was neatly tied on the back of his neck, and he was looking at a smaller woman who was trying to get to him. Her blonde hair floated around her face, but she didn't seem to care, just like she didn't seem to care that her dress was askew. She was trying to get free from the arms of a blond man and a blonde woman who looked remarkably like each other, but they held firm even as she clawed at their arms.

"I will kill you!" she screamed at the tall man. "You killed my son."

"He killed my brother," the tall man said.

From what Loki had explained, Sam could assume who these people were. Vali was the tall man who looked like an asshole, while the woman trying to get to him had to be Frigg.

Sam's heart broke for her. Even though she was a goddess, the pain of losing two sons the way she had must be too much to stand. It didn't matter if she was a goddess. She'd also been a mother.

Tears streamed down her cheeks, but either she didn't care, or she hadn't realized she was crying. Her anger and grief were almost palpable in the air, so much so that Sam could almost feel it himself.

He'd never lost anyone. Well, his grandparents had died, but he'd been much younger, and he hadn't realized what was happening. He'd certainly never lost anyone that would be anywhere close to a son. Still, his heart bled for Frigg.

"What's going on here?" a man with gray hair, a gray

beard, and a bitchy expression asked as he stomped out of the house. "Frigg, what are you doing?"

Drawing attention to himself hadn't been a smart idea on the man's part. Frigg turned around so quickly that the two people holding her almost let her go. She tried to throw herself at the new man—no doubt Odin—but thankfully, the man and the woman caught her again.

"You did this," Frigg spat out. "You killed my son."

"He got what he deserved for killing Baldur."

Loki groaned and rubbed his face with his free hand. "I knew he was an idiot, so I should have expected this," he muttered.

This was too much for Sam. He looked around, needing a distraction. There was a lot to be distracted by, anyway.

The palace they were standing in front of was one of many palaces he could see. They all seemed to be different, as if they belonged to different places and times. Maybe that was the case. He supposed each god changed their home according to what they liked, but it was an odd sight. Everything was beautiful but mismatched.

Then there was the *other* palace. It was massive and behind the others, with tall columns that reached for the sky. It didn't look like a place where people lived, and it made Sam wonder what it was used for.

As he looked around, he realized they were attracting attention. Several people were standing in front of the other palaces, staring in their direction. One woman was coming closer, almost running but not quite. Sam wasn't sure the situation needed more people, but apparently, they wouldn't have a choice.

Sam had no idea what he was doing, and he had no place here, but instead of trying to get away, he squeezed Loki's hand harder and stood tall. Loki needed him, and he'd be there for him, be it the last thing he did.

He just prayed it wouldn't be.

"What's happening here?" Loki thundered, making his best impression of Odin when he was pissed.

At least he got everyone's attention. Frigg stopped screaming, while Odin stared at him as if he were dog shit on the bottom of his shoe. Loki didn't care.

Frey and Freya seemed relieved to see him. They didn't let go of Frigg, which was probably a good idea, and instead, they dragged her closer to Loki.

"Thank the gods you're here," Frey said. "We weren't sure we'd be able to hold her back much longer."

"I'll help," a feminine voice said.

Loki looked up, surprised to see Sigyn. And dammit, she was the last person who needed to be here, considering Sam was present.

What could Loki say, though? Sigyn was his wife, and he hadn't told Sam about her yet. He'd almost forgotten he had a wife, to be honest. He couldn't remember why they'd gotten married exactly, but it had been thousands of years ago. They'd drifted apart almost right away, and they'd had entirely separate lives since then.

Yet, there she was, walking toward Frigg and opening her arms to her. At least Frigg finally stopped trying to get to Odin and Vali and threw herself into Sigyn's arms.

"Vali killed Hodr," Frey said after letting go of Frigg.

"Give me more details."

Frey's gaze flickered to Sam, but thankfully, he didn't ask who Sam was. "I'm not sure what happened when Frigg found Hodr, but I can tell you what I know. Freya and I heard screaming, and we rushed outside. We had to go into Hodr's house, and we found her crying over his body. Vali was there, too, sitting in an armchair and sipping some whiskey." Frey's tone hardened. "He didn't even try to hide the fact that he'd been the one to kill Hodr. He's unrepentant, and when we dragged Frigg out, he followed us. We kept her in our house for a bit, but she snuck out, and we caught up to her here. Vali was here, and he came out of the house to confront her, which ended in the screaming fight you walked in on."

Loki turned his attention to Vali. He looked smug, and like Frey had said, unrepentant. He didn't care that he'd killed Hodr. He didn't care that what happened to Baldur had been an accident. Odin had created him as a weapon, and he did his master's bidding.

"Why did you do it?" Loki asked Vali even though he already knew the answer to that question.

"Because he killed Baldur. I told you I was created for revenge and that I would get it. I'm not done yet, either."

Loki resisted the urge to punch Vali's smug face. So far, no one had said anything about Sam, and Loki didn't want to draw attention to him.

He couldn't deny that Sam's presence was soothing and keeping him calm in a way he hadn't expected. He'd always had a temper, and in a normal situation, he would already have snapped at Vali and probably hit him. The main reason he hadn't today was that Sam was there, holding his hand. He was grateful for Sam's presence, as well as terrified.

He'd known he'd have to confront Vali, but he hadn't expected it to happen this way or for Vali to find out about Sam. He'd never forgive himself if something happened to Sam because of this, but he reminded himself that no matter how strong Vali was, Loki was stronger, and he wasn't without allies. On Vali's side, there only seemed to be Odin. The two of them were powerful, but Loki was positive he'd be able to take them, especially if he had Frigg's help—and she wouldn't hesitate to step in to avenge her sons.

"How many times do I have to tell you it was an accident?"

Loki asked through gritted teeth. "I don't know who gave the spear to Hodr, but he couldn't know what it was made of."

"He still should have known better." Vali took a step forward, but thankfully, he stopped moving again. "You're next on my list, Uncle. Hodr was your weapon, and I took care of him, but now, I'll take care of the brain behind Baldur's death."

Loki wanted to scream. "Why are we talking about this again? I had nothing to do with it, and I wasn't in Asgard when Baldur died." But he knew that nothing he said would convince Vali or Odin. They had their sights on revenge, and they would get it, no matter who they had to mow down.

"But the spear was yours. For me, that's enough."

Loki squared his shoulders. "If you think I'll let you kill me, you're wrong."

"Oh, but I won't do it today. I'll wait until you least expect it, and only then will I strike." His gaze drifted to Frigg, who was sobbing in Sigyn's arms. "But I have to say that I'm surprised you brought your human toy with you, considering your wife is standing there."

Loki felt the shock run through Sam. Sam's back went ramrod straight, and Loki knew that if he looked at him, his expression would be troubled. He waited for Sam to snatch away his hand and demand an explanation, but he didn't. It was confusing but also a relief.

"What do you want, Vali?" Loki asked. He was tired, and he wanted this to be over.

"For you to die. You should have died instead of Baldur, and while I can't bring back my brother, I can avenge him."

"You do realize I'm not Hodr, right? I'm sure you took him by surprise and used the fact that he was blind to your advantage, but you won't be able to do that with me. I'll see you coming, and when we fight, I'll win. You might have been created for revenge, but I'm the god of mischief, and I was born thousands of years before you. I'm one of the most powerful gods in this pantheon, and if you dare try to attack me, you'll have to deal with my wrath."

Loki disliked showing off like this. When he did it, it was usually tricks to make humans laugh. This was different, but maybe it wasn't a bad thing. Maybe it was time for him to remind everyone here that even though he didn't usually use his powers against the other gods, he could if he had to, and he would. If Vali was planning on attacking him, Loki would be waiting for him, and he'd make sure Vali paid for what he'd done to Hodr. Vali's time in Asgard would be short if he continued pushing Loki.

"You're an old god. I don't care about your threats, and you don't scare me," Vali said. "I *want* you to be waiting for me when I finally get to you. I want to look you in the eyes when you realize that I've killed you."

Going after Vali right now wouldn't solve anything. So, instead of jumping him, Loki stayed where he was and stared him down. Vali didn't seem to care, but eventually, he shuffled his feet just a bit. That was enough to tell Loki that he was intimidated even though he acted as if he couldn't care less.

Good. That was what Loki had been aiming for. He wanted Vali to be intimidated. He wanted him to realize that he was poking the wrong god and that he'd regret it if he continued doing so.

Fighting Vali wouldn't bring back Hodr or Baldur, but then nothing would. Now, Loki had to make sure Vali didn't kill someone else for no reason, especially since his name was the next on his nephew's hit list. The best way to make that happen would be to kill Vali, but Loki wasn't sure that bringing more death in the situation would help anyone.

Well, it would certainly help him because Vali wouldn't be after him anymore, and he wouldn't have hesitated to do it before, but now he had Sam to think about. What would Sam think of him if he killed Vali?

Sam wasn't in awe of Asgard anymore. He wasn't even worried about the clusterfuck he and Loki had walked into. No, now he was pissed and sorely tempted to punch Vali in that smug face of his.

Vali was a monster and exactly the kind of god Sam had been avoiding. He was the reason Sam was wary of gods, and while he realized that Sigyn probably *was* Loki's wife, he knew there had to be something that would explain why Loki had never mentioned her and why he was with Sam. Sam wouldn't let Vali get to him. The only reason the asshole had mentioned Sigyn was that he wanted Sam to snap at Loki, and right now, they needed to show a united front.

So even though Sam had about a thousand questions, he stood next to Loki, facing Vali and the others. The blond guy who'd been holding up Frigg was eyeing Sam as if he expected him to blow up, and Sam didn't blame him for it. He wouldn't blow up, though. He wasn't an idiot, and he knew how much danger they were in right now.

No matter what Loki had said before, no matter how angry and dangerous he was, it would still be hard for him to fight both Odeon and Vali on his own. Sam had no doubt that Frigg would get into the fight, and probably the others, too, but he didn't want to risk it. He couldn't risk this becoming an outright war, especially with him in the middle of it.

"This is the last time I'll say it," Loki said slowly. "Stop this madness, Vali. You've killed your brother. Isn't that enough death?"

"He won't stop until he gets revenge on everyone involved in Baldur's death," Odin thundered.

Sam scowled at him, but he was hoping Odin wouldn't notice. Even though Loki had said that Odin wasn't the most powerful god, he was still really freaking powerful, and Sam could admit he was terrified. Odin looked angry, and from what Sam knew, he was a stubborn asshole. He'd never admit he was wrong, especially because he was afraid to lose people's respect. He was convinced Loki was involved in his son's death, and he'd made sure everyone knew that, so he couldn't backtrack.

And there was nothing Sam could do. He couldn't fight a god, not even a minor one, let alone someone like Odin. The only thing he *could* do was stay here, silent, and support Loki in whatever he decided to do.

Which, apparently, was giving Odin and his nephew an ultimatum.

"You don't want to push me," Loki said slowly. "I know you're in pain over losing Baldur. We can all understand that, and I'm sorry you lost two sons to this madness. But you have to remember who I am and what I've done in the past. I've changed, but I won't let you attack me or anyone else. Baldur is already dead, and nothing you can do will bring him back."

"All involved will pay for what they've done," Odin said as if he hadn't listened.

Sam suspected that nothing Loki could say would change that. Odin was convinced he was right, and most men couldn't admit they were wrong. Odin, especially, seemed to be one of those. He was technically in charge of Asgard, and he wanted everyone to view him as powerful and infallible. Sam thought that was the only reason he'd had his second son killed, and he couldn't help but wonder how Odin could sleep at night.

Probably extremely well.

He doubted Odin cared about his sons. This entire situation was more about his honor and getting revenge than about Hodr and Baldur. On the other hand, Frigg was clearly distraught over their deaths, and Sam wouldn't put it past her to get revenge on Odin and Vali eventually. Hopefully, she'd wait until the most challenging part of grief had left her, because otherwise, she wouldn't think straight, and not thinking straight in this kind of situation—going against two gods—could be lethal.

"And that includes you," Odin added.

This fight could have gone on indefinitely, but luckily, Odin turned around and walked back into the house. Vali hovered there for a moment, glaring at everyone, including Sam. Eventually, though, he followed his father into the house. Sam stayed tense, half expecting one of them to come out again to yell at them for a bit longer. When they didn't, he turned to Loki.

"What do you think they'll do?"

Loki sighed and rubbed his face with his free hand. "Nothing good." He turned his attention to Frigg and his *wife.*

Holy fuck, they were going to talk about this as soon as they were home.

"I'm sorry, Frigg," he murmured.

She nodded stiffly. "I know. And I'm sorry you were dragged into this. It was my fault, too. I believed you were involved in the beginning."

"I don't blame you for that. Odin would have tried to involve me even if you hadn't thought I had something to do with your son's death."

"He won't stop until he gets what he wants, and in this case, it's revenge on you."

"I understand, and whenever he strikes, I'll be ready for him. But what about you? I doubt you want to go back into the house with Odin and Vali staying there."

She stepped away from Sigyn and wrapped her arms around herself. "I cannot share a house with them. They killed my sons."

"You can stay with me," Sigyn said in a soft voice.

Sam wanted to hate her, but she seemed like a genuinely nice person. He couldn't help but wonder if he'd ever heard about her, but if he had, he wouldn't be in a relationship with Loki. He wouldn't have given Loki a chance, and he might have regretted it. He had no idea what was going on, but he'd find out, and he was sure Loki had a good explanation.

He better have.

"Thank you," Frigg whispered. Her voice trembled, but she stood with her chin high. "Loki, I'll let you know when they do something. I'm sorry this cannot be avoided, but you know how Odin is."

"I'm going to have to kick his ass this time, aren't I?"

To Sam's surprise, that made Frigg chuckle. "Probably. He's been talking about beating you up for decades. Maybe it's time to show him that won't ever happen."

"Do you need anything? I'll do whatever I can to make this easier on you."

Her smile vanished as she shook her head. "Nothing can make this easier on me. I lost my sons. What am I supposed to do now?"

Sigyn wrapped her arms around Frigg's shoulders and turned her toward the house she'd come from. She smiled at Loki, but thankfully, she didn't stop to talk to him. That would have been kind of awkward. Would Loki have introduced Sam as his boyfriend? Or was he hiding the fact that he had someone else in his life from his wife?

Now that the danger seemed to have passed, Sam wanted an explanation, and he was starting to convince himself that there couldn't be one beyond Loki being a cheater. He didn't want to believe that, and he was convinced it was what Vali had been aiming for when he'd said those words, so instead of stomping his foot and demanding an explanation, he waited.

He didn't have to wait long. There wasn't much for Loki to

do with Odin and Vali gone. Sigyn led Frigg to her palace, while Loki stepped away from Sam to talk to the man and the woman who'd been holding her. He patted the man's shoulder, then came back to Sam and held out his hand. "Let's go home," he said.

Sam was more than happy to do just that. Instead of taking Loki's hand, he wrapped his arms around him, hoping this wasn't the last time he'd be able to do it. If Loki didn't have a good explanation about his wife, Sam couldn't continue being with him, and the thought made him breathless.

He didn't want to lose Loki.

"I know you want to know about Sigyn," Loki said as soon as they were back in Sam's room.

"Please tell me there's a good reason you didn't mention you had a wife? How does no one know about her? I've researched you. I found a lot of information about what you did in the past, but nothing mentioned your wife."

Loki rubbed his face. He looked exhausted, and while Sam felt a bit guilty about pushing him on this right now, he needed an explanation.

"That's because most people don't know about her. I, well, I don't want to be rude, but I'd almost forgotten about her myself. We got married thousands of years ago. I suppose we were both lonely at that time, and we needed each other. It wasn't the best idea, and we started drifting apart almost right away. There was never any animosity or anger between us. I think the last time I talked to her was right after we got married, and neither of us tried to reach the other after that. I think we're both content with our lives now and that even though we're technically still married, it doesn't matter to either of us. I'm sorry Vali brought it up, and I'm even more sorry I didn't tell you about it."

It was hard to imagine forgetting that one was married, but Sam supposed it made sense for a god. He could only imagine the number of things that happened to someone who lived for thousands of years. He could barely remember what he had for lunch yesterday, so maybe it made sense that Loki didn't remember he'd married a beautiful woman thousands of years ago.

Loki was staring at Sam as if he expected him to snap, but Sam had no intention of doing that. He was still there, in Loki's arms, and he pushed up to kiss his cheek. "All right," he said.

Loki blinked. "All right?"

"What do you want me to say? Do you want me to scream at you because you have a wife and you didn't tell me? I was tempted to do just that, but I could tell Vali mentioned her because that was what he wanted to happen. I won't allow this to pull us apart, Loki. You're mine, and I'm not letting go."

The smile Loki gave Sam told him those had been the right words, and he hoped he wouldn't regret them—or being with Loki.

Chapter Seven

Loki tried to be as silent as possible as he puked into the toilet, but it still sounded really fucking loud. He heaved, clutching his stomach because it felt like it was turning itself inside out, and clung to the ceramic bowl. At least Sam kept it clean.

Once he didn't feel like he would die, he took a deep breath, then another. His legs felt like jelly, but he still got to his feet. His knees shook but kept him up, and he flushed the toilet, made sure there were no signs of what had just happened in the room, and washed his hands and face.

He looked at his reflection in the mirror. His long black hair hung around his face, damp from the water he'd used on his face. He was paler than usual, and the shadows around his eyes were darker. He looked tired, which he wasn't used to. He supposed he was, though, and apparently, his body was telling him he needed more rest by making him feel exhausted and his stomach queasy.

He supposed anyone would be tired in his situation. He hadn't gone back to Asgard, but the situation still weighed heavily on his mind. He kept waiting for something to happen because Vali and Odin wouldn't let this go, and his nerves were shot. He was fucking stressed, but he didn't want Sam to realize how badly this was getting to him, so he hadn't told him about any of this or the fact that he'd been regularly puking his guts out.

Loki huffed, pushed his hair away from his face, and straightened his back. Wasting time in the bathroom would make Sam wonder what was happening if he woke up, so it was time to go back to the bedroom.

Loki did so as silently as he could. When he opened the bathroom door, Sam was in the same position he'd been when Loki had shot out of bed, on his side with his front toward the window. The curtains were pulled closed, but a sliver of sunlight still peeked through, illuminating the room enough so that Loki could stare at Sam.

He was beautiful. He always told Loki how gorgeous he was, but Sam was, too. They looked different, but that didn't take away from Sam's good looks. He was more rugged than Loki, broader and more muscled, but that was why Loki liked him. He didn't want an image of himself fucking him, although he'd tried that in the past. No, Sam was perfect for Loki, and Loki was trying his hardest to be perfect for Sam.

He slid back into bed, hoping his stomach had settled for now. Sam grumbled and hooked an arm around his waist, pulling him against him. Loki went with a smile on his lips, knowing that he was safe here in Sam's arms, and he always would be.

"What happened?" Sam asked in his sleep-rough voice.

"Nothing. Needed to use the bathroom."

"Those weren't using the bathroom sounds."

Loki turned around and kissed Sam, relieved he's brushed his teeth before washing his face. Sam wouldn't find out he'd been puking from the stress, just like he wanted.

"I know you're distracting me," Sam muttered into Loki's mouth.

"Is it working?"

Sam didn't answer because Loki was making his way down his body. He paused at Sam's nipples, knowing how much Sam loved it when he bit onto them. He did it hard enough for there to be some pain, but he knew where to stop and how to get Sam to squirm under him.

And Sam did it so beautifully.

They were still discovering what they enjoyed together and how to work their personalities in a way that made it possible for them to be in a long-term relationship. Loki had thought he knew everything there was to know about himself, but now that he was with Sam, he was discovering that wasn't true. Some sides of his personality were surprising even him, like his need to make sure Sam was happy and cared for. He'd never felt that strongly for a human, and sometimes it was overwhelming. Loki had thought it would be too much, but he'd never felt the need to run, and he didn't think he would, not with Sam.

After torturing Sam's nipples for a moment, he continued his path lower.

Sam's hands landed in Loki's hair. Loki knew Sam loved the silky strands, even though Sam had never told him. He always got his fingers in it, which was a dead giveaway and one more reason for Loki to keep his hair long. He enjoyed it himself, and it made him look good, too.

He finally reached Sam's cock. Sam was hard, and while Loki knew what he wanted, he didn't give it to him right away. Instead, he breathed in and out on the top of Sam's cock and waited until Sam couldn't take it anymore.

He grinned when Sam used his hold on his hair to guide him toward his cock. Loki had always enjoyed a bit of hair pulling, and it was delicious when Sam was the one doing it. Loki allowed Sam to slip his cock into his mouth, taking a deep breath before swallowing it down. Sam's hands tightened almost to the point of pain, but that was part of the appeal.

The problem was that it could be distracting. That was also why Loki didn't enjoy sixty-nine much — he could never focus on two things at the same time, especially not those kinds of things. But no one was sucking his hard cock, so that was all right. He didn't even care that he had to hump the mattress, because sucking off Sam was just so good.

Sam smelled of the sex they'd had last night, of sweat, and just a bit of soap. He'd shower again before going to work, but Loki preferred him like this, still sleepy and warm from the time they'd been in each other's arms.

Sam's hips punched up, but Loki hadn't spent centuries perfecting his blowjob skills for nothing. He took everything Sam had to give him, then more as he sucked and swallowed around the hard cock in his mouth and throat. He regulated his breathing and made sure to get enough oxygen, but he had to retreat a bit when his stomach twinged. The last thing he needed was to throw up all over Sam during a blowjob. He'd never live it down, and Sam would get worried.

Loki gave Sam all of his attention, but he wanted pleasure, too. He hooked a leg around one of Sam's and moved so his cock was pressed against the warm, hairy skin. The friction as he thrust against Sam's leg was delightful, almost as much as the cock in his mouth.

Loki was starting to learn the tells of when Sam was about to come. Sam's cock twitched, and he leaked more precum, flooding Loki's mouth with bitter deliciousness. His butt cheeks tightened, and Loki knew it was time.

He sucked hard while pushing a few fingers between Sam's legs. One brush of his fingertip against Sam's hole, along with strong suction, and Sam was coming down his throat. Loki was delighted, and he swallowed everything Sam had to give him as he continued humping his leg. Sam's pleasure was enough for Loki to come, as well, and the skin between them turned sticky with sweat and Loki's seed.

Loki flopped down. He leaned his cheek against Sam's thigh and tried to breathe, but he didn't have much time before Sam hooked his hand sunder his armpits and hauled him up his body. Loki snuggled against Sam's side, sighing in pleasure and ready to get more sleep.

"I'll have to get up soon," Sam murmured against Loki's hair before kissing it.

He seemed to enjoy doing that, and Loki wasn't about to tell him to stop.

"Do you have to go? We could spend the rest of the evening and the night in bed."

"We could, but then I wouldn't be able to pay rent, and I'd get kicked out."

It was on the tip of Loki's tongue to tell Sam he'd pay his rent, but Sam was proud, and he didn't want a sugar daddy. Still, maybe they could find another way to spend even more time together.

Loki would have never thought he'd feel this way for a human, yet here he was, and he wanted to make the most of the time he had with Sam.

Something was going on with Loki, but Sam didn't know what it was. No matter how many times he tried to talk to him, Loki brushed him off, and while in the beginning Sam had put it up to him not wanting to worry Sam, it was too late for that. Sam probably needed to know whatever Loki was hiding, but how could he convince him to talk to him?

They were together, but that didn't mean they owed each other every single secret. Loki especially probably had thousands of them, and Sam wouldn't know how to deal with most of those. Besides, it was probably nothing new. Sam hadn't heard anything new about Odin and Vali, but he had no doubt they were planning something, and that was probably why Loki was so worried.

"How are things going up there?" he asked, hesitant but wanting to at least try.

Loki snuggled closer to him, wrapping one of his arms

around Sam's naked chest. "You mean Asgard?"

"What else could *up there* mean?"

Loki snickered. "I don't know. Your roof?"

Sam swatted him on the ass. "I don't mean the roof, and you know it."

Loki sighed, his entire body moving against Sam's. "I know. I just don't want to talk about Asgard."

"You don't have to if you don't want to, but I'd like to know."

"And you probably should. Odin and Vali know about you, and I'm terrified they'll try to get to me through you. They wouldn't hesitate to hurt a human, and I can't be with you twenty-four seven."

Sam didn't know if there was a solution to this. He gently poked Loki in the ribs, trying to make him smile. "But you'd be with me twenty-four seven if you could."

"I never want to be away from you, but I understand that can be viewed as obsessive, and I don't want you to think I'm a stalker."

"I could never think that." Sam kissed the top of Loki's hair. "You don't know anything else, then?"

"No. Frigg is still staying with Sigyn, and obviously, she's still grieving. Frey keeps sending me texts, but there's never anything new in them. Mostly, he asks about you and our relationship."

"He's the blond man who was there when I visited?"

"You call that visiting? I'm really sorry you had to see my family like that, but yes, that was Frey and his twin sister, Freya."

Sam had imagined they were at the very least brother and sister, but with gods, it was hard to tell. Vali, for example, was only a few weeks old, even though he was a fully grown adult. "You're close to him?"

"Closer than I am to anyone else in my pantheon. He's a

friend, I suppose."

And probably related to him in some way, too. As far as Sam could tell, all the gods were related one way or another. "And why does he want to know about me?"

Loki propped himself up on his elbow and looked down at Sam. Loki was incredible like this, all soft gaze and wild hair. Sam could hardly believe he had Loki in his bed and his life, and he raked a hand through his boyfriend's hair, using the hold to pull him closer and kiss him. Loki hummed into the kiss, clearly more than happy to go along with whatever Sam had in mind.

"Well?" Sam asked after a moment, pulling Loki's face away from his by the hair. He didn't pull hard, but he didn't miss the heat in Loki's gaze. Maybe there would be a bit of hair pulling in their future.

Loki tried to shake his head. "How am I supposed to think and answer a question when you do that?"

"With your mouth. Why does Frey want to know about me?"

"Because I don't usually do humans."

"When you say *do*, you mean being in a relationship?"

"Exactly. I spend most of my time in the human world, so most people I have sex with are humans, but I never enter a relationship with them. I think that's what Frey doesn't understand. He wants to know what happened between us and how important you are to me, but I'm not sure I want to tell him."

"Are you afraid he'll tell Odin and Vali?"

"He wouldn't, but they might still find a way to use the information and you against me. Besides, I don't want him or the others to look at you as if you're a circus phenomenon. They're my family, and you're my boyfriend, which means that eventually you'll probably have to spend time together, but not yet."

Never, if Sam had anything to say about it. His one visit to Asgard had been more than enough for him never to want to go back. It would be nice to meet Loki's family, but he could do without.

"You haven't gone back?"

"I wanted to visit Frigg, but there's nothing I can do for her, and I'd rather stay as far away from Odin and Vali as possible. If anything changes, I might have to go, but for now, I'm more comfortable here." He kissed the tip of Sam's nose. "And I don't want to be away from you."

"You'll have to eventually. I have to go to work."

Loki pouted. "Do you? I could be your sugar daddy."

It was tempting. Who wouldn't at least think about it when they were offered a lifetime of not doing anything and having everything they wanted? Sam didn't know how long they'd be together, and while it would be fun to go around the world and explore without thinking about bills and anything else, Sam didn't want that. He didn't want to depend on Loki entirely, and he already depended on him when it came to his happiness.

"I don't need a sugar daddy. I need a boyfriend," Sam said.

Loki looked like he might protest, but instead, he nodded and kissed Sam again.

But Sam had to go to work. They couldn't stay in bed forever, no matter how much they both wanted to, and he kicked Loki out because he had to shower and get ready. Loki always had things to do, anyway, and when he vanished, Sam took advantage of the situation. He quickly grabbed his phone and dialed a number he hadn't known until meeting Loki.

"Sam?" Jimmy asked when he answered.

"Something's up with Loki."

Jimmy sighed. "I agree, but he won't talk to me."

"I think he might be headed your way." Egypt was where Loki usually ended up when he wasn't with Sam. "But don't push him. I've already asked him what was going on earlier, and we ended up talking about his family and the fucked-up situation they pulled him into, but I don't think that's it, not entirely anyway. He'll clam up if we push too hard, though."

Jimmy sighed. "I know. But I'm worried."

"I am, too."

"I'll try to talk to him, but I won't push."

"I'll do the same again."

"He's so fucking stubborn."

Loki was, and it was one of the reasons Sam loved him. Even though he was a powerful god surrounded by other gods, with humans falling at his feet, Loki was a loner. He only trusted a few selected people in his life, and even with them, he wasn't always entirely truthful. Sam suspected it stemmed from several lifetimes of not having anyone to trust, and while he could understand it, it didn't mean he had to like it. They were both still trying to find their way in their relationship, though, and to find compromises that worked for both of them. Clearly, Loki had to work on being honest with the people who cared about him, but it wouldn't happen overnight.

"He's not staying with you today?" Jimmy asked.

"I'm heading into work, so no."

"I'll be ready for him if he comes here."

"Thank you."

"No, thank *you*. You've made him happier than I've seen him since I've met him. Don't give up on him, please."

Sam had no intention of doing that. Nothing would make him give up on Loki, not his family, not his nephew telling him about his wife, nothing. Whatever happened next, Sam was in this for the long term, even though for Loki, it would be barely more than the blink of an eye. For Sam, though, it was everything.

Loki was everything.

Chapter Eight

Loki should probably be worried that everything in his life seemed to be going well. It had been weeks since he and Sam had gone to Asgard, and there had been no word from Vali and Odin. Frey said they were going on with their lives, and while Loki was still nervous about the fact that they seemed to be giving up getting revenge on him, he'd started to relax. He was feeling better, and his life with Sam was incredible.

All in all, Loki had everything he'd ever wanted, even though he hadn't known he wanted it. He was in a relationship with Sam, he didn't have to play peacemaker in Asgard, and his future was bright.

"Have you seen my red pants?" Sam asked from where he was digging in the dresser.

"Why would I have seen them?"

Sam turned to face Loki. "Because I'm pretty sure I saw them on you the other day."

"They wouldn't have fit me."

Sam arched a brow. "Does it matter? I'm sure you can snap your fingers and make them fit you."

And that was what had happened. Now, they were Loki's, and he had no intention of returning them to Sam. Instead of telling Sam that, he beamed at him and fluttered his lashes. Sam grumbled, but when he turned around again, Loki could have sworn he saw a smile on his lips.

The two of them were basically living together. They went to bed together at night after Sam returned from work, and they woke up together. They spent most of the day puttering around the apartment, going to the grocery store, or doing other things Sam needed to do. Then, when Sam headed to work again, Loki either distracted himself with other stuff or went to Egypt, or he went with Sam. They'd gotten into a routine, and while Loki would have found it boring before, now, he was looking forward to all the little things they did as a couple.

He propped himself against the pillows by the headboard and watched Sam as he got ready. "We should move in together," he declared.

Sam froze for a moment before getting into motion again. "Haven't we already?"

"I suppose we have, but it's not official. Should I pay rent or something like that?"

Sam snorted. "You could probably buy the entire building. But Arlo and Kimberly don't care that you don't pay rent."

"Would they say anything if they did? Or are they still afraid I'll smite them?"

Sam laughed. "Probably a bit. It doesn't matter, though. You've been staying in my room, so you could help me pay my part of the rent, but it's not necessary, especially with all the food you keep buying for us."

Loki liked taking care of people, and Sam and his two best friends, along with Misty the cat, were his family. Loki had been tempted to buy the building, but instead, he limited himself to filling the fridge every time it needed to be and getting dinner ready. It wasn't like he had anything else to do.

"But we could share an entire house," he said. "We could get a dog."

"I don't think Misty would be happy about that."

Loki rubbed the cat's head. She was stretched out on the blankets, acting as if the bed belonged to her. Loki supposed it kind of did, at least when he and Sam weren't in it. "I think she'd get used to it. Or maybe we could get another cat. I like cats."

"I know you like cats. I'm still not sure we should rush into this."

Loki moved closer to the edge of the mattress and swung his feet to the floor. "How would it be rushing? You said that we're living together already. What would it change to live in a bigger place?"

"We don't need a bigger place yet."

Loki opened his mouth to ask when they would because his mind had flickered to children, but before he could, his phone rang on the nightstand. It wasn't Jimmy's tone, but he still grabbed it to see who was bothering him. His eyebrows rose high on his forehead when he saw the name on the screen.

"Who's that?" Sam asked.

Loki tilted the phone so he could see. Sam's eyes widened, and he leaned closer as if he needed to see Thor's name better.

"Why is he calling you?" Sam asked.

"I have no idea, but I'm about to find out." Loki swiped his thumb on the screen and raised the phone to his ear. "Thor?"

Thor and Loki had a complicated relationship. Thor was one of Loki's nephews, and they'd been close in the past, but things had deteriorated between them. Loki supposed they'd grown apart, which wasn't surprising, considering that Thor was also close to Odin.

Which was why this phone call was strange.

"I just heard about Hodr and Baldur," Thor said.

Loki thought about asking him where he'd been that he hadn't yet, but he kept his mouth shut about that. He didn't know why Thor was calling, but he was curious, and he wouldn't get answers if Thor hung up in anger. "I'm sorry you lost your brothers," he said.

"It was a tragic accident."

Loki was relieved that someone else believed him. He hadn't gone back to Asgard and wasn't planning to, but it was nice to know that more than a handful of people believed him. "It was."

The accident still niggled at Loki's mind. He didn't have any answers as to how Hodr had gotten his hands on the spear. He'd tried finding out, but the only one who could have told him was Hodr, and he was dead, killed by Vali's hand. Loki had poked around his house, but he hadn't found anything that could give him information.

"Do you think I could see you?" Thor asked.

Loki blinked. "Why?"

"I just want to talk about what's going on. My father is still on the warpath, and it's worrying. I'm also not sure I like this new brother of mine."

"I doubt anyone likes him. He's kind of an asshole."

Thor laughed. "He probably is. He's my father's son, after all. So? Can we see each other?"

Sam moved in front of Loki. He couldn't hear the other side of the conversation, but he was frowning, and Loki never wanted him to be worried. He quickly lowered the phone, put a hand on it so Thor wouldn't hear him, and explained, "He wants to meet."

"And you think it's a good idea?"

"I don't know. I have no clue what's going on, but he wants to talk about Odin and Vali. Maybe he can give me inside info to make them change their mind."

"I suppose you know him better than I do, but I don't like this."

"That's because you don't like gods in general." Loki leaned forward to kiss Sam's stomach, then raised the phone to his ear again. "I'll meet you," he told Thor.

"Good. I'll see you in Asgard?"

"No. We can meet at a club tonight." That way, Sam would

feel better about Loki and Thor meeting. He was working to-night, and this way, he'd be able to keep an eye on him. Once the meeting was over, Loki could hang around until Sam was done.

"Send me the address."

"I'll see you soon."

"You will," Thor promised. There was a hint of something in his tone, but before Loki could ask what was wrong, he hung up.

Loki blinked at the screen, wondering what had just happened.

"You trust him?" Sam asked.

"Not any more than I trust most gods. We haven't been close in a long time, and things have happened between us."

"I'm aware of that. And he's Odin's son, so he could be working for him."

"I doubt it. Hodr and Baldur were his brothers."

"They're Vali's brothers, too."

"But Vali never knew them. He was created to kill Hodr, and I doubt he stopped to talk to him when he decided to do it. Thor is different."

Or at least, that was what Loki was trying to convince himself of.

Sam didn't like this. He realized he should give Thor the benefit of the doubt since he'd never met him, but while his thoughts about gods had softened somewhat since he'd met Loki and his friends, he couldn't stop wondering what Thor wanted. Could it really be that he wanted to help with this messy situation? Or was there more to it—was Loki walking into a trap?

Sam wouldn't be surprised, which was why he was relieved Loki would be meeting Thor at the club. There wasn't much Sam would be able to do even if they started fighting, but at least he'd be there, and he'd keep an eye on Loki.

He doubted he could change Loki's mind. Loki was stubborn and used to doing whatever he wanted. He'd mellowed some since he and Sam had started dating, but he couldn't change that much over such a short period of time. Besides, Sam wouldn't want him to change. He'd fallen for Loki, and there was no changing the fact that he was a god. Sam had to accept that sometimes, he had to let Loki be, and this was clearly one of those times.

Hopefully, Thor wanted to help, but Sam would have felt better if one of Loki's godly friends had been present. Loki wouldn't call any of them, though, and Sam couldn't betray his trust, so he didn't, either.

Together, they headed out. Sam was glad he didn't have to use public transport anymore, especially when he left the club after it closed. Even when Loki didn't spend the evening at the club, he always took him there and picked him up, almost as if he couldn't bear to stay away from Sam longer than strictly necessary. It was slightly terrifying to have a powerful god's full attention and affection focused on him that way, but Sam didn't see Loki as a god. He was just Loki to him, and he was sweet and gentle in a way Sam couldn't have expected.

Once they were inside, Loki made a beeline for his favorite stool at the bar. It took Sam a few more moments to be ready to start working, and when he stepped behind the bar, it was to find that Loki was already sipping on something.

"Do you think alcohol is a good idea considering what's about to happen?" he asked.

"I'm not going to get drunk. I'm not even sure that's possible. I mean, I could snap my fingers and not be drunk anymore," Loki said. He grinned at Sam. "But it's water."

Sam found himself smiling. He leaned over the counter to kiss Loki's cheek. Then he had to start working, and no matter how hard he tried, it wasn't easy to keep an eye on his boyfriend. He did make sure he was close by when Thor finally arrived, though. There was no way for him not to notice it when the people on the dance floor parted around Thor. Thor was tall, very blond, and he looked around as if he hated being here. Maybe he did. He seemed nice in the movies, but this Thor wasn't the actor. He was the real god, and he might be an asshole, as far as Sam knew.

Thor eyed the stool next to Loki's as if he were afraid he'd get his ass dirty if he sat, but after Loki patted it, he settled onto it. Sam had made a beeline for them, curious to hear the conversation they were having.

"Why this place?" Thor asked, looking around. "It's so full of humans."

The way he said that last word made Sam's eyebrows shoot up. He sound like he didn't like humans very much, which was utterly different from Loki. Sam had started to wonder that Loki wasn't like anyone in his family, and hearing Thor talk like that reinforced that belief.

"Can I get you anything?" he asked Thor when he reached him.

Thor wrinkled his nose. He was a handsome man, but Sam didn't like the spark in his gaze. "Whisky," Thor ordered. "The best quality you have, although I doubt you have much in this place."

Sam gritted his teeth. The club wasn't his, so he shouldn't be offended by Thor's dismissive tone.

"You're being a bit of an ass," Loki said. He winked at Sam, and Sam found himself smiling, even though he was irritated. Loki could always make him feel better, and tonight wasn't any different.

Sam delivered the whisky to Thor, but he couldn't hover close even though he tried. He was called to the other side of the bar by one of his coworkers who needed help, and by the time he turned around again, both Loki and Thor were gone.

He looked around, hoping they'd gone to the bathroom, or maybe that they were dancing, but he couldn't see them. He walked toward their spot to grab the glasses, and his eyes widened when he saw a ring next to Loki's glass.

He picked it up and held the still-warm metal in his hand. Why had Loki left his ring? He loved those things, and he had several on both his hands. He never left home without them, and this one especially, if Sam remembered right, was precious to him. It had been a gift from Jimmy and Qebui to thank him for pushing them together.

He would never have left it behind.

Something was wrong. It had to be for Loki to leave the club without telling him and leave the ring. That meant he had to find Loki, but that wouldn't happen unless Loki was still in the club somewhere.

"Hey, I've got to use the bathroom," he told his coworker.

"Just be quick," she said before turning back to a customer.

Sam rushed away from the bar. He checked the dance floor, then the bathrooms, but Loki was nowhere to be seen. His last resort was to go to Idris, and even though this might get him fired, he didn't hesitate to rush to the office. The door was closed, but his boss told him to come in when he knocked, and he did it so quickly that he tripped and almost fell on his face.

"Sam?" Idris asked, sounding confused as he started to rise from his seat behind his desk.

"I know I'm supposed to work right now, but I think something happened to Loki."

Idris cocked his head. "The two of you are close."

"We are, and he was meeting his nephew at the club tonight, but they're both gone, and I know something happened. Do you think I could watch the CCTV footage?" It was a gamble, but Idris would want to know what happened to Loki, too.

Thankfully, Idris didn't hesitate. "Come around the desk."

Sam obeyed and held his breath as Idris clicked around on his computer. He opened a window, and the club appeared on the screen. Another few clicks and the people on the dance floor started moving. Sam found Loki quickly, and he watched as he and Thor talked. The quality was shit, but he could see that at one point, Loki started frowning. Then Thor grabbed his arm so hard that Sam wouldn't be surprised if he left bruises. He leaned closer, whispering something in Loki's ear, then he looked at Sam. He said something else, and Loki nodded, then got to his feet. Sam watched him as he fiddled with his rings, then reached for his glass and took one last sip of water. When he put the glass back down on the counter, the ring glinted next to it.

Thor hadn't let him go during all of this, and he pulled Loki along. He was dragging him, which was a sure sign that Loki hadn't gone with him willingly.

He'd been kidnapped, and there was nothing Sam could do because he wasn't a god.

Loki shouldn't have followed Thor out of the bar, but Thor had threatened Sam, and Loki didn't want to risk it. He'd been suspicious when Thor had called, and now he knew he was right, but unfortunately, that didn't help his position. He was in trouble, and he didn't know how to get out of it.

"You don't look happy," Thor said as they reached the lake where they used to spend time when they were still friendly.

"You threatened Sam," Loki pointed out, glaring at his nephew.

"I just wanted to make sure you'd come with me. I didn't know there was something between the two of you. Who is he?"

"None of your business. What do you want?"

Thor rocked back on his heels and stared at Loki. "Why did you do it?"

"Why did I do what?"

"My brother. What did he ever do to you?"

Loki groaned. "Not you, too. I hoped that you wanted to talk to me because you had more sense than your father, but clearly, I was wrong."

"Don't talk about him that way." Thor's tone was threatening, but Loki wasn't afraid.

"Did he tell you I had something to do with Baldur's death? Because I didn't. The spear might have been mine, but it was supposed to be in my house, and I doubt Hodr knew about it. Even if he had, he wouldn't have gone in my house."

"You gave it to him."

"I didn't. I'm not even sure where the spear was."

"In the closet in one of the guestrooms."

It took Loki a moment to realize what Thor's words meant. "Are you the one who gave it to Hodr?"

Thor grinned. "No one will believe you even if you try telling them. They're all convinced you were the one who did it, and that was how I wanted things to go."

Loki tried to ignore the sense of betrayal filling his chest. He and Thor weren't close, but he still hadn't expected something like this from him. "Why?"

"Because something needed to be done about you. It's time you pay for everything, and what better way than to have Odin kill you himself?"

"If that was what you were going for, you failed."

Thor shrugged, seemingly uncaring. "Doesn't matter. I still have you here, and it's over for you."

"You're going to try to kill me?"

Thor grinned. "And I won't be the only one."

Just as he finished talking, more people appeared. Loki wasn't surprised to see Vali, and he should have expected

Skadi, since he'd killed her father a while back, but he *was* surprised to see Sigyn and Frigg, at least until he realized they were here to try to stop the others. Frigg looked like an avenging angel, and while Sigyn seemed out of place, she was still here, and it mattered.

Thor grabbed Loki's arm. He squeezed to the point of pain and held out his other hand. In it, he was holding a small bottle. "Drink," he ordered.

"I don't think so."

"You'll drink if you don't want the people I left back at the club to hurt your human."

From Thor's expression, Loki could tell he'd do it. Loki would survive whatever was in the bottle, but Sam could get hurt. Even if Loki went to him now, he might not be fast enough.

He did the only thing he could do—he took the bottle. The liquid inside was transparent and didn't taste of anything when Loki drank it. He didn't feel anything, either, but he didn't fool himself into thinking that wouldn't change.

Loki faced the other three as he dropped the bottle. "What do you think you're going to do?"

Vali grinned. "Wouldn't you like to know?"

Loki would, but he didn't expect any of them to answer. He tried to think quickly, wondering what he could do. Fighting them was an option, but there was only one Loki and three of them. Frigg and Sigyn could help, but they weren't anywhere as strong, especially Sigyn. As for Frigg, she was grieving, and Frey had told Loki she hadn't been eating much. Loki didn't want to have to rely on either of them, and he didn't want them to get hurt.

So, it was only him.

Since fighting was out of the question, Loki had to run. He was afraid to leave Frigg and Sigyn in case the three dumbasses decided to take their revenge on them, so instead of vanishing into thin air, he shifted.

Many people forgot that Loki was a shifter, and he didn't use the ability as much as he had once. Now, though, it came in handy, and Loki turned himself into a fish and threw himself into the lake.

He'd swum here when he was younger, but never as a fish, and it had been thousands of years. He wasn't sure where he was going, but he tried to rush away from the three as quickly as he could. He found a bunch of rocks at the bottom of the lake, and he wiggled his way between them, hoping it would be enough to hide him until the three got tired of trying to get to him.

It was fun to watch them try for a bit. Skadi found a net somewhere, and they threw it and caught fish after fish— none of them Loki. Unfortunately, Thor knew one of Loki's weaknesses now. He stood at the edge of the lake, his hands on his hips, and bellowed, "Do you want me to go get your boyfriend?"

"The human?" Vali asked.

Loki swore. Sam wouldn't be able to do anything against them, so Loki had to find a way to keep them away.

Loki doubted they'd kill him if they caught him, even though he had no idea what they were planning. Whatever it was, it wouldn't be good for him, and it would take him away from Sam, but maybe it was a price Loki was ready to pay to keep him safe.

He was afraid Sam wouldn't understand why he'd suddenly vanished, but he had to take a chance if it meant Sam would be safe, even if he was angry at him for the rest of his life. Loki would do everything to get back to Sam, but he had to deal with this first and see what happened.

Maybe he could try to get past them. He wiggled away from the stones and slowly made his way to the edge of the lake. He looked exactly like a fish from the outside, and he hoped the three would confuse him for one. He wasn't the only fish around, and he tried to hide between the others, but unfortunately, Thor had always been good at seeing him when he was shifted. They'd played a lot when they were younger, and now, it was coming back to bite Loki in the ass. He was also feeling faint, which couldn't be good.

Thor pointed at him in the water. "There. Get him."

Skadi stepped forward with the net, but Thor tore it from her hands and threw it into the water. Loki jumped, trying to get over it, and two warm hands wrapped around his tiny fish body. Thor squeezed, pushing the breath out of Loki's body. He raised Loki and stared him in the eyes. He looked like a giant, and Loki didn't like that, just like he didn't like anything in this situation. "Got you," Thor murmured.

Loki shifted back—what else could he do? He tried to leave, but nothing happened. Whatever Thor had given him was working, and too well.

Thor grabbed his arm while Vali kicked him in the back. It hurt, but Loki managed to kick Vali back, hitting him right behind the knee and sending him to the ground. He laughed, sounding slightly manic and not caring one bit.

Thor gave him a good shake and dragged him toward the mountain wall by the lake. Sigyn and Frigg followed, but they didn't do anything useful. While Frigg was trying to talk some sense into Skadi, Sigyn was wringing her hands.

"He had nothing to do with my son's death," she said. "Why are you doing this?"

Loki knew the answer. They were doing it because they wanted to. Thor had decided Loki had offended him a while ago, and he'd sworn he'd get revenge for that. Apparently, this was his way to do it.

With Thor's hand firmly clamped on Loki's arm, Loki couldn't even leave. He'd just take Thor wherever he was going, and that wouldn't end well. He still tried, but Thor hit him in the face, making the world around him tilt and go black around the edges.

When Loki came back to himself, it was to see that Thor had dragged him into a cave.

He swallowed and looked around. He was pretty sure he'd explored this place when he was younger, but it had been too long for him to remember anything useful. He was relieved when Thor threw him against the wall, at least until Vali grabbed him and pushed him onto his back on a flat stone. He tried to resist, but he could do nothing while the three tied him up to three rocks he was stretched upon. There was one under his shoulders, one under his butt, and one under his legs, and no matter how much he pulled on the bonds, he couldn't get free.

The three assholes stood above him. Vali and Thor were grinning like loons, and while Skadi wasn't, she was happy with what they were doing.

Sigyn tried to throw herself on top of Loki, but Thor grabbed her and pushed her against the wall. Loki struggled against his bonds, but he couldn't move.

"Don't touch her," he said through gritted teeth.

Vali arched a brow. "So you still care about her, even with your human toy?"

"Shut your mouth," Loki spat out. It wasn't the most original of retort, but he couldn't think of anything better at the moment. "What are you going to do to me?"

Thor's smile widened. "You're about to find out."

Sam rushed out of the club before he could think about what he'd do next. He stopped in the middle of the sidewalk, looking around as if something on the street could help him decide.

He had to save Loki, but how? He didn't know where Loki

was, and even if he did, what could he do against a god like Thor? No, the only people who could fight a god were other gods, and Sam wasn't one.

But he knew some.

He took out his phone with a trembling hand and dialed the first number he thought of. It took Jimmy a moment to answer, and when he did, he sounded happy. "Hey," he said. "What are you and Loki up to? Do you think you might want to visit?"

"He's gone," Sam croaked.

There was a moment of silence, and when Jimmy spoke again, his tone was completely different. "What do you mean, he's gone?"

"He was meeting Thor at the club. He wasn't supposed to leave with him, but I was working, and by the time I turned around, both of them had vanished. Loki left a ring for me on the counter, and he'd never have gone away without it. Something's happened to him, and we need to save him."

"Where are you?"

"In front of the club."

"Stay where you are. Qebui is coming to get you."

Jimmy hung up, and Sam sucked in a breath. He wasn't surprised when Qebui appeared next to him almost instantly. He rushed toward him, grabbing his arm. Qebui's expression was grim, but he didn't ask what had happened. Instead, he whisked Sam away to Egypt.

The change in temperature was shocking, but Sam didn't care. He clutched the ring in his hand and looked around, hoping to find someone who could help him.

Qebui had taken him to Jimmy's office. Jimmy had been pacing in front of his desk, but he rushed to Sam as soon as Sam appeared. He grabbed Sam's arms and gave him a little shake. "Tell me what happened."

"I don't know. Thor called Loki while I was getting ready

for work. He said he'd heard what happened with Hodr and Baldur, and he wanted to talk about it. He didn't believe Loki had something to do with it, and Loki was happy about that. He agreed to see Thor, and he decided they'd do it at the club so I wouldn't freak out. I left them talking at the bar, and when I came back, they were just gone, and this ring was next to Loki's glass."

Sam opened his hand so that Jimmy could see the ring. Jimmy sucked in a breath when he did so, most likely because, like Sam, he knew Loki wouldn't abandon the ring. He gently touched it, but he didn't take it away from Sam, instead closing Sam's hand around it again.

"Do you have any idea where they went?"

"No. I watched the CCTV, and I think Thor threatened me so that Loki would follow him, but there's no way for me to be sure. I have no idea what's going on, but I know we have to get him back."

"You said Thor heard what happened with Hodr and Baldur. What does that mean?"

Sam swore. He'd forgotten that Loki had kept his friends away from the mess in Asgard. The only reason Sam knew about it was that they'd spent so much time together, and it would have been impossible for Loki to keep it a secret from him.

He raked a hand through his hair. "Hodr and Baldur are Loki's nephews, Odin's sons. Loki told me that they were playing around, and Hodr was throwing stuff at his brother. I don't know the entire story, but Baldur could only be killed by a weapon made of one specific kind of wood. Loki had a spear made of that wood in his house, and somehow, Hodr got his hands on it. He used it against his brother, and Baldur died." Sam had to stop and swallow. His mouth was dry, but when Jimmy offered him a glass of water, he shook his head. He wanted to get this over with as soon as possible, which meant he had to finish his explanation.

"Odin was convinced Loki had something to do with it, and I guess it's understandable, but Loki swore he wasn't in Asgard, and he didn't even remember the spear. It was a gift or something like that. Anyway, Odin went nuts, and he had another son. Vali was created to get revenge for Baldur, and he killed Hodr."

Jimmy sucked in a breath. "But Hodr was his brother and Odin's son."

"They didn't care about that. He's dead, and I'm afraid that Odin decided to go after Loki now. He still blames Loki for what happened, even though Loki had nothing to do with it."

"What about Thor? What does he have to do with this?"

"I have no idea." Sam sighed. "Today is the first time I heard about him from Loki. Loki said they hadn't been close in a long time, but he still trusted him enough to meet him, and obviously, to follow him away from the club."

"Maybe it wasn't trust," Qebui said. "Maybe he left with Thor because Thor threatened you. That's what you think happened, isn't it?"

"From what I saw on the CCTV, yes. I think he took Loki. I think that somehow he's involved and that he's on Odin and Vali's side." That meant they were up against three gods, and Sam had no idea how to help Loki.

He moved away from Jimmy and Qebui and started pacing the way Jimmy had been when he'd arrived. "What am I supposed to do? Those three are gods, and if Odin is involved, it's even worse. I can't do anything to help Loki. I'm only human. I can't fight a bunch of gods, not if I want to make it out alive." He'd sacrifice himself to save Loki's life, but he suspected Loki wouldn't want him to.

They needed to have a good talk once all of this was over, and Sam would tell Loki he loved him and that he was ready to move in with him officially. He didn't care that it was fast.

He didn't care about anything but Loki, dammit.

A hand on Sam's shoulder made him stop moving. Jimmy's smile was sad, but he still tried to reassure him. "We'll get him back."

"How?"

"You and I might be human, but we're not alone. Loki doesn't just have us, Sam. He has Qebui, Sed, and a whole bunch of Egyptian gods, and I'm sure he has friends in other pantheons, too. He probably has friends in his pantheon, and we just have to contact them to find a way to get to him. He has enemies, but he also has people who care about him, and they'll all want to help."

Sam wanted to believe him, but he was afraid to. "How do we get them to help?"

"We'll go to the sky palace first," Qebui said. "Nu will want to know about this."

"You think they'll want to be involved?" Jimmy asked.

Sam tried to remember who Nu was. He was sure Loki had mentioned them, but he couldn't remember much beyond that.

"You know how close they are to Loki. If something happened to him, they'll want to know about it and help."

"You think they'll be the only one?" Sam had to know, even though he sounded rude.

Qebui looked at him. "I doubt it. For one, I'll be there. I might be only a minor god, but that doesn't mean I can't fight."

"I never meant to offend you."

"You didn't offend me. But I think we all realize that we're going up against powerful gods, which means we need powerful gods on our side. That's not me, but it doesn't mean I can't be involved. Loki is Jimmy's best friend and one of my friends, which means I'll save him, whatever I have to do to make it happen."

Sam sucked in a breath. "All right. Let's do this."

He didn't care how many gods they had to get together, they were going to save Loki, and they were going to do it now.

Chapter Nine

L oki had hoped Vali and Thor would be done with him once they'd tied him up, but he should have known better. Vali hovered there, peering down at Loki while looking delighted.

"Do you know what those bonds are made of?" he asked.

Loki looked down. The bonds were rough, and he'd assumed they were rope, but now that he looked better, he realized they weren't. He'd seen many things over the thousands of years he'd been alive, and the sight of those ropes made his stomach churn.

He didn't answer, but that didn't stop Vali. "You see, we knew we had to make them extra strong. Normal ropes would have been too easy for you to break. Narvi's entrails, on the other hand, are strong enough to keep you here for eternity."

Loki sucked in a breath and looked sideways at Sigyn. She seemed shocked for a moment, but it wasn't long before she wailed. Loki desperately wanted to go to her, to apologize for what had happened to their son, but he couldn't move. The only thing he could do was glare at Vali, but Vali didn't seem to care.

"He fought back," he said. "But we were stronger than him, and now, he'll keep you here for the rest of eternity."

Loki pulled on his bonds, and even though the feeling of them moving on his skin made him want to throw up, it didn't stop him from trying to get free. Vali was right, though. He couldn't get them to budge, no matter how hard he tried.

He was horrified. He loved all his children, even though he didn't have contact with most of them. After thousands of years, families tended to drift apart, and Loki's wasn't any different. But he still grieved Narvi, and Sigyn was, too.

Vali leaned over Loki, so close that Loki could smell him. "This is why my father created me. He wanted me to torture you, to make you pay, and now, you'll have the rest of your immortal life to think about what you've done. You won't ever leave this place. This is your punishment, and I can't tell you how happy I am that you'll finally pay for what you did."

Loki almost told Vali that he'd had nothing to do with what happened to Baldur, but it wouldn't work. It hadn't before, and he was starting to realize that Vali probably didn't care about the truth. He was enjoying both having Loki at his mercy and torturing him, which meant that no matter the truth, he wouldn't stop.

"What have you done?" Frigg asked.

Thor turned to her. "You need to leave."

"Haven't you heard me when I told you that Loki had nothing to do with Baldur's death?

"The only reason I haven't hurt you is that you're my father's wife, but if you try to intervene, I *will* stop you."

Instead of being cowed by Thor, she stood up straighter and stared right at him. "I lost my two sons. I'm the one who lost the most here, and neither you nor your father should have a say in how revenge is taken."

"They were my father's sons, too."

"They were, but *you* never cared about either of them. You're using them as an excuse to get what you've always wanted, and I won't allow you to do that."

Thor stood up straighter, and even Loki would have been intimidated at his glare. Frigg trembled, but she stood firm and faced him.

"Be careful what you say," Thor gritted out. "Considering everything that happened, I doubt my father will care if I kill you."

She opened her mouth, but Loki shook his head, hoping she'd notice. He thought she did, because she didn't say anything and instead took a step away. She looked ready to kill, but that wouldn't happen.

Loki thought the worst had already happened until Skadi stepped into the cave. She was holding something in her hands, and when Loki saw what it was, he knew that the punishment Thor and Vali had come up with would be even worse than what he'd expected.

"What are you doing?" Sigyn asked. She tried placing herself between Loki and the others, but one push from Vali, and she was slammed against the wall. She hit her head, and a trickle of blood marred her pale skin. Frigg was by her side instantly, glaring at Vali, but the two of them were too smart to try anything else.

Loki watched as Skadi walked up to his head. She placed the snake just above Loki's head without hesitation, and the animal hissed. Loki watched as a pearl of what he suspected was venom dropped from one of the snake's fangs. It hit him in the forehead, and pain exploded in his entire face. He could feel the venom eating at his flesh, and even though he didn't want to give Vali and Thor the satisfaction, he screamed.

Someone screamed with him, but he couldn't tell whether it was Frigg or Sigyn. A soft hand touched his cheek, and he blinked his eyes open to see Sigyn leaning over him. Someone, no doubt Frigg, had tried cleaning the blood on her forehead, but there was still a trace of it.

"You can't do this," she said with a sob.

"We can do whatever we want," Vali answered. "And if you try to free him, you'll have to answer to Odin. Now go. We need to seal him in."

This was even worse than what Loki had expected. They were going to leave them here, along with the snake, for eternity. The snake's venom would continue to drip on Loki's face, and he'd continue being in pain.

And there was nothing he could do about it.

He pulled on the bonds again, barely caring about the fact that they were his son's entrails. If he allowed himself to think about it, he'd break down, and he couldn't do that now. He had to get free and go back to Sam.

Who was to say that Vali and Thor wouldn't hurt him with Loki out of the picture? Sam would be safe if he stayed with their friends, but would he know to do that? He had no idea what happened, and while he was probably angry, Loki had no doubt he'd try to find him. It would be impossible for him to do so, no matter how much he tried, and Loki's heart broke for him and the pain he'd feel.

Thor grabbed Frigg's arm and pushed her toward the exit, but when Vali tried doing the same to Sigyn, she slapped him. He jerked back, then reached for her again, obviously pissed, but Skadi grabbed his shoulder. "Let her. She wanted to be married to him, and now, they can spend eternity together," she said with a snarl.

Loki was going to wring her neck the next time he had the possibility.

"You need to go," he told Sigyn. "I'm pretty sure they'll close off the cave, and you'll be stuck with me here."

She dried the tear that rolled down her cheek. "What does it matter? I lost my son. I have nothing else to live for but my husband."

Loki wanted to tell her that wasn't true, but she was mourning, and he couldn't take that away from her. She knew what she was going against if she stayed, and as they both listened to something heavy being placed in front of the cave entrance, he was glad he wasn't alone.

Then, another drop hit his forehead. He screamed more freely this time, not caring one bit who heard him. Sigyn's hands were soft on his cheeks, but she couldn't do anything about what was happening on his forehead, or at least, Loki thought so until he blinked his eyes open once the worst of the pain had faded.

Sigyn stood above him, a stone bowl in her hands. She'd placed it just under the snake, so the next time one of the drops fell, it would fall into the bowl. Loki didn't know where she'd gotten it, but he could imagine she'd created it using the stone that surrounded them.

"What are you doing?"

"Helping you." Her gaze drifted down Loki's body. "We need to get you out of here."

"We won't be able to."

"I'm sure your boyfriend will find you. He'll want you back before the birth."

Loki frowned. It hurt his forehead, so he stopped instantly, but he still didn't understand what Sigyn meant. "The birth?"

"You're pregnant, aren't you?"

Loki stopped breathing. Was he pregnant? It wouldn't be the first time, but it wasn't something that happened often, so he hadn't thought about it, even when he'd started getting sick. He'd blamed it on the stress of what was happening with Vali and Odin and on something he'd eaten, but now that Sigyn had pointed it out, he could see why she thought he was pregnant.

He raised his head and looked down at his stomach. He wasn't the kind of person who stared at his reflection in the mirror often, and he'd been so busy that even when he showered, he didn't pay much attention to his body. There was a small bump there, though, and its presence explained why he'd been so sick.

He was pregnant, and if no one came to save him, he'd give birth tied up in this cave—and Sam would never know he had a child.

Sam was freaking out, and he couldn't do anything to stop. Things were moving, but not fast enough, and considering how long Thor had had Loki already, Sam had no doubt Loki had been hurt. He wanted to scream at the people around him to get a move on, but one look from them could smite him, and he didn't want to risk it.

Everyone was here to help Loki. The problem was that they didn't know where to start. It had been hours, and the last person who'd seen Loki and Thor was Sam. He had no idea where they'd gone, and he didn't know how to find out.

He raked a hand through his hair and peered out the window. He was tempted to go into the garden, but he didn't want to miss one word of the conversations happening in the room.

"I know it's useless to say it, but you should relax," Sed said.

Sam glared at him. "Would you be able to relax if your boyfriend had been taken?"

"No, but then, he's human. Loki is immortal, so even if they hurt him, he probably won't die."

It was that *probably* that worried Sam. "Gods can be killed. The death of one of Loki's nephews is at the root of all of this."

Sed nodded. "We can die, but it's quite hard to kill us. Besides, from what you said about Vali, I think he'll want his revenge to be as long and painful as possible."

"So you think he's torturing Loki?"

Sed grimaced. "Probably, although I wasn't planning on telling you that. I suck at reassuring people."

"I don't want to be reassured. I don't want to be lied to. I want the people here to tell me the truth about what's going on, and I don't care what the truth is. Loki needs me, and it won't help him if I hide my head in the sand."

Sed lightly inclined his head at Sam. "I understand, and I

apologize. Yes, my guess is that they're torturing him, and while it sounds and *is* bad, it's also a good thing, because it means they're keeping him alive."

"But we don't know how long they'll do it."

"We don't need much longer."

Sam was skeptical. He looked at the gods gathered around him. Qebui had brought him and Jimmy to what Jimmy called the sky palace. Sam hadn't known what to think of it when he'd realized it was the place where the Egyptian gods lived. Instead of being made up of several big palaces like Asgard, it was one colossal palace where all the gods lived. It was impressive, but Sam didn't have time to look around and play tourist. No matter how much in awe he was, he needed to focus on Loki.

Once at the sky palace, they'd gone to see Qebui's ancestor. They and Loki had been friends for a long time, and when Sam had explained what had happened to Loki, they'd been angry. Only a few orders from them, and gods had gathered in their living room.

Sam didn't know most of them. When he'd met Loki, he'd gone over what he knew of the Norse gods, but he hadn't explored the Egyptian pantheon. He knew Qebui and Sed, of course, and now Nu, but that was where his knowledge ended.

"We should head out," Nu declared, looking around. "Ra, you're coming with us."

Sam had heard the name before, and he wasn't surprised to see it belonged to a tall man with reddish-blond hair. He bowed curtly, even though Sam knew he was one of the most powerful gods in the Egyptian pantheon. Yet Nu ordered him around as if he weren't.

"We're not going to end up with another fight on our hands, are we?" he asked Sed as he leaned closer.

Sed looked confused. "Who would fight?"

Sam gestured between Ra and Nu. "I mean, I know Ra is powerful."

"He is, but even he has a family. Who do you think Nu is?"

"I have no idea because no one told me."

Sed nodded. "They're the creator of the Egyptian pantheon. By that, I mean that they were the first Egyptian god. They gave birth to Ra, Amun, and Atum. They're Ra's parent, and he's always respected them. He'll go to war if they ask him to."

It was reassuring to have such a powerful god on their side. Well, *gods,* since Nu was coming with them. Sam couldn't help but wonder how Loki had become their friend, and he'd make sure to ask when he had Loki back.

But first, he had to make that happen.

Of all the people coming along, he was the only one who wasn't a god and who didn't have powers. Jimmy had wanted to come, but Qebui had pointed out that he wouldn't be able to focus if he had to worry about Jimmy's safety. Besides, there was nothing Jimmy could do to help Loki, and when Jimmy had argued that Sam was coming, Sam had asked if he'd stay back if Qebui had been the one taken.

Jimmy had grumbled, but he'd agreed to stay back after Nu had talked to him. He'd made them promise to call as soon as Loki was safe, and Sam had gone along with it, even though he suspected he'd have other things to focus on when that happened.

"What's our first step?" he asked, looking around the room.

Along with him would be four gods. He hoped it would be enough to keep Thor and Vali at a distance and that no one would get hurt. He wanted Loki back, but he'd never forgive himself if something happened to these people.

They weren't just gods to him. He'd gotten to know Qebui especially, and he liked the guy. It was easy to forget that the people standing around him were gods when they treated him like he was one of them. He'd never felt that way about gods before, and just like he'd changed Loki, he realized Loki had changed him.

"We have to find out where he is," Nu said.

They stroked the head of a weird mummified cat that had been twining around their ankles since Sam and the others had arrived. Sam had wanted to ask what was up with the cat, but he didn't dare. He also wanted nothing to do with the thing. It was just too weird for him.

"How can we do that?" Sam asked.

"Who would know what Thor is up to?"

"Well, his father probably would, but I doubt Odin will tell us anything. Maybe his wife?"

"Didn't she believe Loki had something to do with her son's death?" Jimmy asked.

"In the beginning, but she changed her mind. She knows Loki had nothing to do with it, and at this point, I don't think anyone else could know what's going on. At the very least, we should try to talk to her."

"That means invading another pantheon's home," Qebui said.

Nu stood up straighter. "Then that's what we'll do. They took one of us, and I don't take that nicely."

"He's not one of us," Ra murmured.

Nu glared at him. "He might as well be. He might not be part of our pantheon, but he's my friend, and I'll do everything I can to save him. I've been his family more than his ever has been, and he should have come to me when all of this mess started. He didn't, and now, I'm going to have to save his ass."

It was good to know they wouldn't stop in front of anything to get Loki back, but Sam couldn't help but worry.

What if no one knew where Loki was?

"I have to empty the bowl," Sigyn said. She sounded panicky, as if she were afraid to displease Loki.

The snake's venom had started dripping more quickly over the past hour, and the bowl was already full. It meant that if she stepped away to empty it, at least a few drops would land on Loki's forehead, which wouldn't be great. However, there was nothing either of them could do to change the situation.

Loki forced himself to smile at her. "It's fine."

"You'll be hurt."

"And it won't be your fault. Do what you have to do."

She nodded, and her expression set. She turned her attention back to the snake, and as soon as the next drop fell into the bowl, she quickly stepped to the side and turned it upside down against the wall. It sizzled and smoked, the acid eating at it as if it were nothing more than butter — or Loki's flesh. She was as quick as possible, but the next drop landed on Loki's forehead.

Loki gritted his teeth and screwed his eyes shut in an attempt not to scream. He didn't want Sigyn to feel guilty for what was happening because she had nothing to do with it. If she hadn't decided to stay with him, he'd be entirely alone, eaten by the venom dripping on his face. As it was, she'd sacrificed a lot to be here with him, and he didn't feel he deserved it.

She placed the bowl under the snake again, and Loki sucked in a deep breath.

"Thank you," he whispered. If given a chance, he'd heal from this, but that chance seemed further away as the time passed.

Sigyn looked down at him. She was pale, and her lower lip trembled. "You're my husband."

Loki wanted to cry. "I still don't deserve what you're

doing. I abandoned you."

But Sigyn didn't seem offended or angry. Instead, she smiled. "Maybe you did, but I didn't have a problem with it. I think we got married for the wrong reasons, and we both knew it. I was lonely, and I wanted someone in my life. You gave me our son, and that was enough for me. I'm sorry to tell you this, but I never loved you, and I never wanted anything more from you."

It didn't offend Loki. If anything, it made him feel better. "You were happy?"

Her eyes filled with tears, and she looked away. "Until Vali killed my son. I don't know what I'll do now. We were close, and even though we drifted apart over the decades, he was still my son."

"I'll make sure the people who hurt him pay for it."

Sigyn shook her head. "But don't you see? That's the kind of revenge that created this situation."

Loki hadn't yet had the time to think about what Thor had done. He didn't want to believe that his nephew had snuck into his house, looked around for the mistletoe spear, and had given it to Hodr. He'd been planning this all along, but Loki didn't understand what his goal had been. Was it this? To have Loki tied to these stones, closed off in a cave forever? But why?

Loki and Thor hadn't been close in a long time, but they'd never been outright enemies. They poked at each other, but Loki hadn't realized Thor hated him so much, and to use his own brothers to make this happen?

That bit didn't surprise Loki. Odin and Frigg were married, and their two sons were the *official* ones. On the other hand, Thor was the son of one of Odin's mistresses. He was one of many. Even though everyone knew who his father was, maybe he felt it wasn't enough. Maybe he'd been jealous of his brothers, and he'd decided to kill them.

It would have been strange for a human to do this, but for a god? It was everyday business. That was one of the reasons Loki disliked spending time in Asgard. Most gods were nuts, and he wanted nothing to do with them.

He supposed he wouldn't have any contact with gods in a long time if he was stuck in this cave.

"Tell me about your boyfriend," Sigyn said.

Loki found himself smiling even though there was nothing about the situation to make him smile. "His name is Sam. He's human."

"I'm aware of that. Are you happy with him?"

"I am. I should have talked to you about him before, and I'm sorry you found out the way you did."

"Stop apologizing to me. We might be husband and wife, but we both know there were never any feelings between us. I don't care that you have a boyfriend. I only care that your human makes you happy." She leaned closer, but not so close as to jostle the bowl she was still holding. "You're one of the few gods in Asgard who's always treated me right. I'm a minor goddess and most gods don't care about me, but it doesn't matter. I just want to be respected, and you did that. I never regretted marrying you or leaving you behind. I never regretted having your son. It doesn't matter that we drifted apart and that we were never truly together. I want us to be friends, Loki, especially since we might spend a lot of time here together."

Loki found himself smiling back, because what else could he do? Sigyn had always been strong, and he was glad she didn't hold a grudge against him. It would have been her right to, but she was a better person than him.

"Tell me about your Sam," she ordered softly.

So Loki did. He told her how he'd met Sam and how Sam had treated him differently than most humans. He explained that was why he'd been so interested and why he'd pursued

Sam until Sam had given in and agreed to go on a date with him. His voice shook a few times, and his eyes prickled with tears at the thought that he might never see Sam again, but he went on until his mouth was dry and Sigyn had to step away to empty the bowl again.

The venom burned, eating at Loki's skin and muscle. It was one of the most painful things Loki had ever been through, and he swore to himself that if he ever got his hands on Vali, he'd make sure the god knew what it was like to be in this position.

"And the child?" Sigyn asked after she was back in her position.

"Would you believe me if I told you I'd forgotten I could get pregnant?"

She chuckled. "I would. It hasn't happened often, has it?"

"But I knew it was a possibility. It's just that I wasn't a woman when I was with Sam. I was always in this form, and I'm not sure how it happened."

Sigyn gently reached out and patted Loki's stomach. "Maybe it was destiny. However it happened, I know you and your Sam will love this baby."

Loki wanted to touch his stomach and feel the life growing there, but he couldn't move. "I don't know if we'll ever get out of here."

"We will. You have to keep hope. From the way you talk about him, it's clear Sam loves you, and even though he doesn't know about the baby, he'll come for you."

"He's only human."

"Does it matter? Do you doubt that he's doing everything he can to get to you?"

"I'm sure he is." And Sam wasn't the only person who was looking for Loki. There was Jimmy, which meant that Qebui was there along with him. Qebui was a god, and he could do more than Sam and Jimmy put together. If he was smart, the first thing he'd done was to contact Nu. They were one of the most powerful gods Loki had ever met, and if they stepped in, Loki had no doubt he'd be out of the cave soon.

He looked down at his stomach. Would Sam be happy about the baby? Or would he be freaked out? Loki wouldn't blame him for it. Sam always avoided talking about Loki's children, especially Sleipnir, although that was probably because of what Sleipnir was rather than the fact that he was Loki's son.

They hadn't talked about the future or having a family, but now they'd have to, and Loki found himself both dreading the moment and feeling excited about it. If he lost Sam because Sam didn't want the child, he'd be destroyed, but he'd deal with it. He was going to be a father again, and even if Sam was out of the picture, he'd honor Sam by raising their child the right way.

But first, he had to get out of here.

They were headed to Asgard. Sam wouldn't have been able to reach the place if he'd been on his own, but Qebui, Sed, Nu, and Ra didn't have any problem getting him there. It didn't seem to bother them that they didn't belong to the pantheon who lived there or that they would no doubt be unwelcome. Nu especially was on the warpath, and Sam was glad to be on their good side.

He guided them toward the house where he knew Odin lived, hoping Odin wouldn't be there. They needed to get to Frigg, but he wasn't sure where to find her. The only palace he knew in Asgard was this one, and he crossed his fingers that nothing would happen.

He stared at the palace in front of him. "How do we do this?"

"Don't have anyone else to call? Maybe someone who'd

know where to find Frigg?" Qebui asked.

Jimmy hadn't been happy about staying back, but it had been for the best. Sam would never forgive himself if something happened to Loki's best friend, and it was one fewer person to worry about. Still, maybe he would have been able to contact someone, because Sam couldn't think of anyone. "I know Loki is close to a few minor gods, but I wouldn't know how to contact them."

"I don't think you'll have to," Nu said. They were looking in the distance, and when Sam squinted in that direction, he realized two people were rushing toward them.

He hoped that whoever was coming wasn't about to attack them, but he still readied himself for it, even though there was nothing he could do to defend himself or the others.

Luckily, he didn't have to. When the two came closer, he recognized the twins, Frey and Freya. He allowed his shoulders to relax, even though Frey especially looked frantic.

"What are you doing here?" he asked, looking around as if he expected Odin to burst out of the house at any second.

"We're looking for Frigg," Sam said, stepping forward.

"She's not here. She hasn't been staying here since she lost her sons."

"Do you know where she is? We need to talk to her."

"It's about Loki and what those assholes did to him, isn't it?"

Sam swallowed. "Do you know what they did?"

"Come with us. Frigg is staying at our home so you can talk to her there."

It was more than Sam expected, and he was relieved to be able to walk away from Odin's palace.

Their small group followed the twins to a smaller, nicer-looking palace. This one looked more like a home, and Sam was more comfortable, but he wasn't here to make friends. He was here to find out where Loki was, and he marched into the home after Frey and Freya, intent on demanding an answer from Frigg.

They found her in the kitchen. She was sitting at a wide wooden table, sipping on a steaming mug. She got to her feet when she heard them, and her eyes widened when she saw who had come with Sam.

"What is the meaning of this?" she demanded to know, drawing herself as tall as she could.

"Do you know where Loki is? Thor took him, and I haven't seen or heard from him since then," Sam said. He realized he was rude, but at the moment, he didn't care.

Frigg's expression changed. "And you came all the way to Asgard to ask me about this? You're human."

"But I'm not," Nu said, stepping forward. "I know I don't have to introduce myself for you to know who I am. Tell us where Loki is if you know. If you don't, point us in the right direction, and we'll take things from there."

Frigg hesitated, and, before she could say anything, the front door slammed open. All of them except for Nu and Ra jumped, and Frigg looked around frantically, her eyes widening when three men walked into the room.

"You don't belong here," Odin thundered, pulling himself up as he stared down at Nu.

He was terrifying. His white hair was wild around his face, and he looked like he could kill someone with nothing more than a glance. He probably could, too, and Sam was amazed that Nu didn't seem to care. Sam was shaking in fear, and it was too easy to imagine what Odin could do if he turned his attention to him.

"We're here to help Loki," Nu explained.

"The traitor is paying for everything he's done. I won't let you get to him."

Nu arched a brow. "I wasn't asking for your permission."

Sam had been amazed when, still at the sky palace, they'd

gone from being middle age to a much younger person. They looked like a warrior now, and he had no doubt they could kick Odin's ass without breaking a sweat. He hoped it wouldn't come to that, because he doubted that a war between pantheons could end up well for anyone involved, but he was willing to risk it if it meant saving Loki.

Frigg slammed her hands onto the table, making her mug jump. "Shut it," she snapped at Odin.

"How dare you," Odin spat out.

Frigg pointed a finger at him. She stepped toward him, but she still kept her distance. She was a smart woman. "Because of you, my sons are dead."

"I had nothing to do with Baldur's death."

"Maybe not you, but your sons certainly did. I heard Thor tell Loki he was the one who gave Hodr the spear. He knew it would kill Baldur, and he did it on purpose." Frigg glared at Thor, who didn't seem one bit worried about her accusations. "They took him to the lake where Loki enjoyed spending time when he was younger," Frigg said, turning back to Nu. "I can take you there or tell you how to reach it. He's sealed in a cave, so you'll have to get him out."

"That won't be a problem," Nu promised.

"You can't take them there," Odin said. He sounded slightly panicky, which wasn't something Sam thought was possible.

"I'll do whatever I want, and you'll keep your mouth shut and stay out of it," Frigg told him. "I lost my sons because of you, and if you even try to stop me, I'll make sure you pay for that. And you, too," she said, turning our attention to Thor and Vali. "You're lucky I don't kill you. You might not be afraid of me, but I'm still a powerful goddess, and I'm much older than you. Don't push me, because you won't like the results."

Vali was looking around as if he wasn't sure how to react,

but Thor didn't try to get to Frigg. Maybe there was some truth in what she'd just said, but Sam still hoped one of them would do something stupid. He wanted to see someone kick their asses since he couldn't do it himself.

"I'll take care of them," Frigg promised. "I have no doubt that at least one of them will try to stop you because they're idiots, but I'll make sure they don't intervene."

Nu curtly bowed. "Thank you. And I'm sorry for your loss."

Frigg's expression shifted to grief and sorrow. "I'll never get my sons back, but if I can help someone, I will. Loki had nothing to do with this, and he shouldn't be paying for it."

Frigg explained where they could find Loki. Sam wouldn't have been able to do any of this if he'd been on his own, and Loki would be stuck in that cave forever. It would take them a bit to get him out, but they would, and soon, he'd be free.

"Let's go," Nu said once they had all the information Frigg could give them.

"You'll regret this," Odin yelled.

Nu didn't even look at him. "I'll make sure you regret it if you ever raise a finger against Loki again. I don't care who you are. Loki has powerful friends in several pantheons, and you're lucky we're the only ones who came today. If you try to hurt him again, you'll find out about the others, and you'll regret it."

There was a finality in their voice that even Odin seemed to recognize. He didn't try to stop them again as they left the palace, but Sam only fully relaxed once they were out.

"Now what?" he asked, looking around.

Nu smiled at him and offered him their hand. "Now, we go get Loki."

Chapter Ten

"This damn snake is going to leave scars," Loki bitched.

Sigyn glared down at him. "But at least you'll be alive. Or do you want me to step away?"

"Of course not." Loki sucked in a breath. "I apologize. I'm in pain, tired, and hungry."

Sigyn smiled. "I remember how it was to be pregnant. Just, please, can you stop being so bitter? I understand you're losing hope, but this isn't going to help either of us."

Loki sighed. She was right, and he shouldn't be taking all of this out of her. She was the only one who'd stayed back to help him, even when she could have easily left. She didn't owe Loki anything, no matter what she believed. Yet she was here, the only one helping Loki, and he'd be forever grateful to her. He'd be forever grateful to anyone who came and helped them, but so far, no one had arrived.

He had to keep hope. Sam was coming for him, but of course, it was complicated. No one but the people who had stuck Loki in this cave knew where the cave was and what had happened to him. It would take Sam and whoever came with him to rescue Loki a while to find out about this place. Then once they were here, they'd have to unseal the cave.

But so far, Loki hadn't heard one whisper of someone out there helping him. It was hard not to lose hope, especially when Sigyn had to step to the side to empty the bowl and the venom dripped on Loki's face. No matter how much he twitched this way and that and tried to get away from under the snake, he couldn't move enough to make that happen.

Sigyn straightened, and her head snapped toward the cave entrance. "Did you hear that?"

"The only thing I hear is my stomach growling. I'm hungry," he whined.

Sigyn glared at him. "Stop listening to your stomach and *listen.*"

Loki swallowed and did just that. He had no idea what he was listening for, and his eyes widened when he recognized footsteps and voices. "Someone is out there."

"I told you they'd come to rescue you."

"What if instead of Sam, it's Thor and Vali?" Loki wouldn't put it past them to come back and gloat and watch him writhe in pain. It was precisely the kind of thing they'd do.

Sigyn frowned. "Why would they come back?"

"Why would they do any of this? I don't know, and I don't think it matters. It could be them, though."

She looked torn, and Loki understood.

"I have to put down the bowl," she said.

"Just step to the side. If it's Thor and Vali, they'll leave you be if they can focus on me. You don't have to get hurt for my sake."

Sigyn's glare deepened. "Shut up. I'll sacrifice myself if I want to. My life is not yours to decide. It belongs to me, and if I want to attempt protecting you, I will." She hesitated. "But I have to put down the bowl. I'm sorry."

"Don't be. I would be in much more pain if it weren't for you. Do what you have to do."

She stared for a moment longer before nodding and setting down the bowl. To Loki's surprise, she put it right on his forehead.

"You can't move," she said. "As long as you stay as still as possible, it won't fall. I just emptied it, so it won't be full for a bit, and hopefully, I'll get to it before it starts dripping."

That wasn't something Loki wanted to experience, and he

hoped for his sake that she was right.

Even though it was one of the hardest things he'd ever done, he stayed as still as possible as Sigyn placed herself between him and the cave entrance. She was ready to defend him, and he promised himself that if he got out of this cave in one piece, he'd make sure not to isolate her the way he had before. They might not love each other, and even though their marriage didn't mean anything to either of them, she was a good person. She could become a friend if Loki allowed it, and he had every intention of doing just that.

The footsteps came closer, and they were rushed. Loki tensed as someone burst into the cave. He couldn't see who it was because Sigyn was in front of him, but the moment she stepped aside, Sam was rushing toward Loki.

"The bowl!" Sigyn yelled.

Sam slowed down. He was visibly horrified as he took in the snake and the bowl on Loki's forehead. He reached for it, but he didn't touch it as if he were afraid to hurt Loki. Loki couldn't look away from him, though.

"You came for me," he whispered.

Sam knelt next to the stones where Loki was tied up. "Did you think I wouldn't?"

Sigyn picked up the bowl again and raised it to the snake. Loki tilted his head so Sam could kiss him, but he couldn't move any more than that. Sam's gaze roamed over Loki's face, pausing on his forehead, which was no doubt ruined by the venom, but Sam didn't seem to care. He kissed Loki, and though it was brief, it was enough for Loki's chest to expand.

Sam had come for him. Sam was rescuing him, and soon they'd both be out of here.

A tug made Loki look down. Sam was trying to loosen the ties around him, but he couldn't. Sigyn made a wounded sound as she watched him, but neither of them told Sam what the bonds were made of. Sam would have been horrified, and it was a pain Loki didn't want to inflict on him.

"You just had to get yourself kidnapped, didn't you?" Nu said as they strolled into the room. They sounded as if rescuing other gods from caves where they were tied down with their children's entrails was something they did every day.

They stared down at Loki, and their gaze snagged on Loki's stomach. Their lips curled into a smile, and before Loki could say anything, they said, "I see congratulations are in order."

"What are you talking about?" Sam asked. He was still tugging on the bonds, trying to free Loki. "Get him out of here, please. That snake is still dripping venom all over him."

Sigyn was holding the bowl again, making sure the venom didn't drip in Loki's face. They had a bit of time, but Loki couldn't wait to be free.

Nu's eyebrows rose high on their forehead. "Why didn't you tell us about this?"

"Tell you about what?"

"The baby."

Sam froze. He wasn't looking at Loki, and Loki desperately needed him to. He had to know what Sam thought of the baby and if he was about to lose the man he loved.

Sam finally looked over at Loki, blinking. "What are they talking about?" he asked.

Thankfully, Qebui stepped forward. He grabbed the bonds and pulled, and though they moved, they didn't break.

"We need the venom," Sigyn said. "But I don't want to remove the bowl from under the snake."

The snake was still dripping venom, but it wasn't looking at Loki. It was staring at Ra, and when Ra gestured with his hand for the snake to move sideways, it obeyed. Loki gaped as he watched it, but then his attention was pulled away. Sigyn was dripping the venom from the bowl onto the bonds while Nu tugged at them until they snapped.

Loki jerked into a sitting position and wrapped his arms around himself. Sam was there, holding him in a sitting position as far away from the snake as possible. Sigyn finally put down the bowl, looking relieved.

"Loki?" Sam asked.

"We should probably head out," Nu said. "We're all happy to see you're okay." They wrinkled their nose as they stared at Loki's forehead. "Although that's going to take a few days to heal. I can help, if you want."

"I can take care of it," Loki promised. "And thank you." He looked at the other gods in the room.

He'd expected Nu and Qebui, and maybe even Sed, but Ra was a surprise. He looked bored as he poked around the cave, finally making his way to the snake. When Ra reached for it, the snake hissed, but it allowed the god to take him. It wrapped around Ra's forearm, looking as if it were nothing more than a pet, and certainly not like it had been spitting venom on Loki's forehead until a few seconds ago.

"Loki? What was Nu talking about?" Sam asked.

Sam sounded panicky, and Loki knew he wouldn't be able to avoid explaining what Nu had been talking about. He just hoped Sam wasn't about to freak out and run.

Sam needed an answer to that question, and he needed it now, because what he thought was happening couldn't be possible.

Loki shuffled his ass until he was on the edge of the stone he was sitting on. He swung his legs to one side, leaning harder against Sam.

Sam allowed him to. He wanted Loki to know he could rely on him, always.

"I didn't mean for this to happen," Loki said. He got to his feet, and he moved as if he were about a hundred years old.

Sam didn't move away but instead helped him steady

himself. His forehead was a mess of burned flesh, and while it turned Sam's stomach to look at it, he didn't try avoiding it. This had happened because of Loki's family, and he needed to remember that the next time they were in front of him.

Not that Sam would be able to do anything to them. He was weaker than even the most minor god. But he'd remember who had betrayed Loki and who had been on his side.

"I'm pregnant," Loki explained. He wasn't looking at Sam and instead was staring at the cave wall. "I'm not sure how it happened."

Sam snorted. "I'm pretty sure you can imagine how it happened."

"I know it's because we made love, but I wasn't supposed to get pregnant. I was in this form the entire time, and it shouldn't have the equipment necessary to birth a child."

Sam hesitated. "It's not going to be a problem for you when the time comes?"

Loki slightly turned to face Sam. He was worried, and Sam wanted to reassure him, but he didn't know if he could.

He'd never expected Loki to get pregnant, even though he'd known it was a possibility. He'd thought that even when Loki had been pregnant, it had been on purpose, but maybe he should have known better. Who in their right mind would want to carry a horse's child?

Sam didn't know how to feel about the baby, but he knew how he felt about Loki. He wasn't leaving him, not unless Loki wanted him to.

Loki shook his head, and his entire body tilted to the side. Luckily, he was slim enough that Sam didn't have a problem holding him up. "I'll be fine. I'll change my body when the time comes, and it won't be a problem. But what do you think about it? We never talked about anything like this, and I'll understand if you want to leave."

"I'm not going anywhere."

Before Sam could add anything, like the fact that he was in love with Loki and he couldn't imagine his life without him, the sound of rushing footsteps made all of them freeze. They turned as one, facing the entrance of the cave, and Sam wasn't surprised to see Thor, Vali, and a blonde woman walk in. Odin was nowhere to be seen, but these three could probably create enough problems for their little group.

"We won't allow you to take him," Vali snarled.

He didn't hesitate to throw himself at Qebui. Sam sucked in a breath, but he couldn't leave Loki behind, and even if Loki had been healthy what was Sam supposed to do against these gods?

So he did the only thing he could. He helped Loki walk toward the back of the cave, then sit down again on the stones he'd been tied to. The bonds were still there, lying on the ground, and Loki avoided looking at them for some reason. Maybe it gave him too many bad memories.

The gods were a sight to behold as they fought. Sam didn't think he'd ever seen this kind of fight between gods, let alone powerful ones like Nu and Thor. Thunder made the cave rumble and shake under Sam's feet, and lightning crashed to the ground, making Sam jump.

Loki wouldn't be able to defend himself in his state, so Sam placed his body in front of him. Loki's wife had been with him when Sam and the others had entered the cave, and she did the same, knocking her shoulder against Sam's.

Sam didn't know what to think of her, but he was grateful that Loki hadn't been alone through all of this. He trusted Loki, and he believed him when he'd said there was nothing left between him and Sigyn. She was still a friend, though, and she was clearly ready to defend Loki right along with Sam.

Sam just hoped he wouldn't have to step into the fight, because he doubted he'd win.

Sam gaped as he watched Ra use the snake he'd picked up

earlier against the woman who'd come in with Thor and Vali. She danced away from him, but the venom of the snake splattered against her chest. She screamed, and Sam watched in horror as the skin of her chest started melting.

"She deserved that," Sigyn murmured.

"It's still horrible to watch," Sam said.

Sigyn nodded. "But Skadi was the one who brought in the snake. She knew what she was doing."

"Why did they do this?"

"Because they feel they have a good reason to," Loki answered. He sounded sad and exhausted, and he was clutching his stomach as if it hurt. "I killed Skadi's father. I'm not proud of it, and it happened thousands of years ago, but she has her reasons to hate me."

Sam stepped closer, but he still kept his back to Loki. "Are you okay?"

"I don't know. Physically, I'm as fine as you can imagine after what I went through, but I feel like all of this is my fault."

"And you're right," a strong voice said.

Sam turned to find himself face to face with Vali. He swallowed heavily, but even though he wanted nothing more than to run away screaming, he stayed where he was and stood strong in front of the god. It wouldn't take Vali much to kill him, but he'd have to do that if he wanted to get to Loki. Sam wasn't just defending the man he loved anymore. He was protecting his child, and he'd do everything he had to do to make sure they came into the world, even if it meant he never met them.

"Loki didn't deserve any of this," he said.

Vali snorted. "Do I have to remind you why I was born, little human? I'm here because of revenge. I'm here to punish Loki."

"You're here because you're an asshole. It doesn't matter why you were created. It doesn't matter what your father wants from you. You're an adult, and you should make your own decisions. The fact that you decided to torture Loki tells me that you're not a good person and that you're a slave to what your father wants. You don't have a mind of your own, and once Odin is done with you, he'll throw you away, and he'll never think about you again. How will you deal with that?"

To Sam's surprise, Vali took a step back. Sam had known he wouldn't be able to do anything to stop the god physically, but he'd hoped that some of the things he could say would hurt him. Apparently, he'd nailed it.

"Odin won't ever let me go." Vali stood up straighter. "He created me. He worked with me."

"Only because you could give him something he couldn't do himself. I won't allow you to hurt Loki."

"Did you research him when you started sleeping with him? Do you know what he'll bring into the world eventually?"

Sam swallowed heavily. "I've read the prophecies."

Vali cocked his head. "And you don't care about that? You don't care that Loki can bring down Ragnarok and the end of the world as you know it?"

"Why should I care about old dusty prophecies? Loki will never do anything like that, and if he ends up destroying the world, it won't be his fault. Instead of trying to kill him over that, or rather, instead of using it as an excuse, maybe you should try to find a way so Ragnarok doesn't happen."

"I've had enough of you, little human. It's time for you to either step aside so I can reach Loki or die with him."

Sam tightened his hands into fists. Sigyn tried to step in front of him, but Sam pushed her away. He was terrified, but he wasn't afraid of Vali. Whatever the god threw at him, he'd deal with it.

Even if it meant he had to die.

Chapter Eleven

Loki wouldn't allow anyone to hurt Sam, least of all Vali. Sam wouldn't be able to defend himself since he was human, so Loki hooked an arm around his waist and pulled him to the side.

He wasn't surprised when Sam tried to stay where he was and glared at him, but he couldn't afford to let Sam be hurt. He'd never forgive himself.

Loki tried to stand taller, but his entire body hurt. His forehead was on fire, and he needed to wash the venom off because it continued eating at his skin, but no one was offering him a bottle of water to do so, and besides, he'd been through worse. Like always, he'd survive, and he'd be stronger by the time all of this was over.

"I won't let you hurt him," he told Vali.

The asshole laughed. "And what are you going to do? You can barely stand on your feet. Or do you think the human will defend himself? Because let me tell you, I doubt it'll do him any good."

"I might be weak, but I'm still more powerful than you, and I'll show you that."

Vali rushed forward. Loki braced himself for the punch that was coming, since Vali seemed to enjoy brawling like a human, but it never came. A hand shot out, grabbing Vali's fist and stopping him in his tracks.

Ra stood there, looking like an avenging angel with red hair, the snake still twined around his forearm. The snake hissed at Vali, who stumbled back when a drop of venom landed on his forearm. Ra let go, looking bored, while Vali's eyes were wide as he tried to clean off his arm.

"You're not so strong anymore," Loki said.

Vali glared at him. "Your place is here, and I won't allow anyone to take you out."

Loki had hoped that once Vali, Thor, and Skadi realized they were outnumbered, they'd let it go, but he should have known better. Vali had been born for this. He'd spent all his time since he came into the world with Odin, who had twisted his mind until Vali couldn't think of anything but revenge.

Loki didn't want to kill him. He just wanted to make sure he and his family would be safe, and that meant he had to get Vali away from them.

His gaze fell on the stones where he'd been tied down. He looked up at Ra, who still hovered close, and Ra seemed to understand what Loki was thinking about. He nodded, and Loki knew they could do this. On his own, he wouldn't have had a chance. With Ra and the others, though, he'd win this fight.

He stepped forward, but a hand on his forearm stopped him. "What are you doing?" Sam asked. "You can't fight with him. You're pregnant." He'd stuttered on the last word, making it clear he wasn't used to thinking of Loki as pregnant, and it was endearing.

"Being pregnant doesn't mean I'm weak," Loki told him.

"No, but you were just tied to a stone for hours, without being able to move and with venom dripping on your forehead. You haven't eaten in all the time."

Loki couldn't deny he felt shaky, but he could do this. "I'm not facing him alone," he promised.

Sam stared at him for a moment. He clearly wanted to stop Loki, and Loki was surprised when he let go and nodded curtly. "Fine. Do what you have to do, but if he tries anything, I'll kick his ass myself. I'll also drag you out of this cave and back home and tie you to the couch until the baby is born."

The thought of being tied down again should have terrified Loki, but Sam just wanted to take care of him. Even though he was still trying to wrap his mind around the fact that they were having a baby, he'd accepted it, and he wanted to take care of Loki and their child.

Loki leaned forward and kissed Sam's cheek. "I'll be fine."

Then he stood up as straight as he could, ignored the burns and pains making his body ache, and moved toward Vali.

The other god was on his feet again, but every time he tried to step away, Ra stopped him. The snake on Ra's forearm hissed and spat, and Loki made sure to stay as far away from it as he could. He didn't fancy being burned anywhere else, although he wouldn't mind sticking the snake on top of Vali's face like Vali had done to him.

Vali cocked back his arm when Loki reached him, but this wasn't the first time Loki was in a fight, and it wouldn't be the last. He threw himself at Vali before Vali could punch him, sending both of them to the ground. He managed to grab Vali's head as he did so, and he slammed it back. Vali's skull made a loud sound as it hit the stone, and it was both stomach-churning and satisfying. Vali wouldn't die from it, but that wasn't Loki's goal anyway.

He slammed Vali's head to the ground a few more times until someone squeezed his shoulder. When he looked up, Ra offered him his hand. Luckily, it was the hand free of snake, and Loki took it and allowed the other god to haul him to his feet.

"Ready?" Ra asked.

Loki nodded. Each of them grabbed one of Vali's arms, and together, they dragged him toward the stones. Vali had to be dazed, because he didn't try to resist until Ra picked him up and stretched him out over the stones. Then he started to wiggle, and it was satisfying to stop him by punching him on his smug face. Loki's knuckles hurt, but he'd take the pain if it meant being able to punch Vali.

Vali continued to struggle, sending blood everywhere, but between Loki and Ra, with some help from Sam, who had realized what they were doing and had picked up the bonds, they tied Vali to the stones where Loki had been lying until a few moments ago. It was harder than it had been for Loki because the bonds had been burned and were shorter, but they made it work. Once Loki was sure Vali wouldn't be able to get out, he stepped away and looked down at him.

Vali struggled, his face red. "You can't do this!"

"I can, and I just did it. You're lucky I'm not asking Ra to put the snake back in place. I'm tempted, but I'm not as cruel as you and the others. You can stay here without the snake until someone comes to rescue you."

Loki couldn't help but wonder if anyone would. Odin wouldn't care. Once he found out Vali had failed in his revenge against Loki, he'd wash his hands of his son. Thor probably didn't care about his half-brother, either. Just like Odin, he'd used Vali.

Now that Vali had been taken care of, Loki turned his attention to the rest of the cave. Skadi was slumped against the wall, curled onto herself as she tried to protect her burned chest. Loki winced because he knew how much it hurt, but he wasn't sorry the venom had burned her. She'd been the one who brought in the snake, and it was savagely satisfying to see her hurt by it.

Thor was still standing, but he was facing Nu, Qebui, and Sed. Once Ra and Loki joined them, he seemed to reconsider attacking them. He wouldn't have won against Nu and the other two, and he certainly wouldn't now that five gods faced him.

He spat on the ground. "This isn't over," he threatened.

"As far as I'm concerned, it is," Loki told him. "I never

want to see you again. We were friends when we were younger, but that's over after what you just did to me. Don't ever come to me if you need anything, and if I see you, I'll make sure to remind you of how angry I am. You'll come out of any encounter we share on the bottom and in pain, so you better stay away from me."

"You wouldn't be threatening me if your friends didn't surround you."

Loki smiled. "I wouldn't, but I don't need them to kick your ass. But see, that's the difference between you and me. You're alone. Your allies don't care about you, and they won't try to protect you if I attack you. On the other hand, my people love me, and they'll do anything for me, including standing up to you. You won't win, Thor. You might as well stop trying. And if I ever see you again, you'll pay for everything that happened today."

Right now, Loki had better things to focus on, and he wouldn't put his baby in danger, but he wasn't lying. If Thor ever darkened his doorstep, Loki would make sure he could never do it again.

Sam could have cried once they finally exited the cave. For a moment, he'd wondered if they ever would. The fight had been hard to watch, especially when Loki had stepped in. Sam had been terrified that something would happen to him, mostly because he wouldn't have been able to do anything. He was only human, and he was surrounded by gods.

It was foolish to think that he could ever compare to any of the people around him right now, and he supposed he should get used to being around gods. He was in love with Loki, and with the baby coming, Sam knew the others were part of his life now. It was intimidating, but he supposed he'd get used to it.

He was holding Loki up as they left the cave. Thor had stormed out a few moments earlier after Loki had threatened him, and Sam was glad he was nowhere to be seen. Vali and that woman were still in the cave. She would probably free Vali, but Sam didn't care. As long as Vali stayed away from them, the man could do whatever he wanted. But Loki had been clear. He'd get rid of Vali or anyone else who tried to threaten his family ever again.

"You need to see a doctor," Sam told him as they left the cave. He blinked, trying to get used to the sunlight. It was brighter than it had been when they'd entered the cave.

"Have you ever heard of a god going to the doctor? I'll be fine," Loki promised.

Sam glared at him. "How can you say that? Even if you ignore the burns on your forehead, don't you need to see someone for the baby?"

Loki's expression shifted. "You've accepted the fact that I'm pregnant quite easily."

That wasn't true, but Sam would fake it until he made it. He didn't want Loki to worry about him accepting the pregnancy, and besides, he wasn't about to leave Loki. That meant accepting he'd be a father. "Why wouldn't I? Were you lying to me?"

"I'd never lie to you, especially not about something so important. I'm not a hundred percent sure I *am* pregnant, though."

"So you need to see a doctor."

"I don't want to go to Asgard."

Sam agreed. He never wanted to see Asgard again, even though Loki had a home there. They couldn't move into Sam's apartment, especially with the baby coming, so they'd have to find another place, but if Sam had anything to say about it, Loki was never going back to Asgard.

"Come home with us," Nu said.

They looked older again now that the fight was over. It confused Sam's brain, but he'd get used to this and much more if he was going to hang around gods.

"Isis or Thot will be happy to make sure you're okay," Nu continued. "I'd avoid Sekmet, though."

Sam leaned closer to Loki. "Who are those people?"

"Gods of healing," Loki said with a smile. "But Sekmet is also the goddess of war and disease."

"It would be great if we could avoid war for the next few months," Sam agreed. He turned his attention to Nu. "And we'll come, thank you. I want to make sure Loki is okay."

Nu stared at him for a moment, and Sam could tell he was being judged. He stood up straighter, praying he wouldn't be found lacking. He had no doubt that Nu would step in if they thought he wasn't good enough for Loki.

Eventually, they nodded. "It was about time you found someone to take care of you," they told Loki.

Loki's arm around Sam's shoulders tightened. "I didn't think I needed anyone, but Sam proved me wrong."

Sam was exhausted and wanted nothing more than to go home and get into bed for the next week, but first, he had to take care of Loki. He allowed Nu to take both him and Loki back to the sky palace, where a tall, very thin man with black hair and a beaky nose checked Loki over while Sam sat at a table nearby.

He was almost asleep with his head on the table when a gentle hand stroked his hair. Sam blinked up to see Loki standing next him. His forehead was fully healed, and he wasn't as pale as he had been before.

Sam sat up, trying to clear the sleep from his brain. "The doctor is done with you?"

Loki nodded, and when Sam pushed away from the table, he wiggled his way onto Sam's lap. Sam wanted to go home, but he was more than happy to sit here with him for a while since Loki needed this. He wrapped his arms around Loki and held him close, his heart finally believing Loki was safe.

"I'm sorry about your family," he murmured.

"It hurts a bit to lose Thor, since I thought he was still my friend, but they don't matter. I have a new family now."

"And Nu will kick the ass of anyone who even thinks about hurting you."

Loki kissed Sam's jaw. "They will, but they're not who I was thinking about. I have you and our baby now."

That gave Sam a jolt. "So it's confirmed? You're pregnant?"

"I'm definitely pregnant. Thot made me pee on a bunch of cereal, and he says he'll be able to tell us if it's a boy or girl in a few days."

"What?"

Loki shrugged. "It's a thing ancient Egyptians did. Don't ask me how it works, because I didn't have the energy to find out."

"I don't care how it works." But Sam wouldn't say no to finding out if they were having a boy or girl. Not that he cared, but he hoped it would help make the baby more real in his mind.

He knew Loki was pregnant. He understood that, and he understood what it meant, but he couldn't imagine them as a family yet. He couldn't picture himself as a father, and he was terrified he wouldn't do a good job.

But he'd try. He wouldn't abandon Loki and their child, no matter what happened.

"Take me home," Loki whispered.

Sam smiled. "You're going to have to do that. I can't exactly take you around the world the way you do."

"Let's go, then."

Sam gently squeezed the back of Loki's neck. "You said goodbye to everyone?"

"I have, and I told them not to visit. I need to sleep for a week."

"That's what I was thinking, so I'm all for it." Sam would have to find a way to deal with his job, but then, he supposed he'd have to find a way to make it work once the baby arrived anyway. Right now, he was too exhausted to even think about it, so he was glad when they suddenly went from sitting on a chair in the sky palace to being on his bed.

He flopped back, ready to sleep even though he wasn't comfortable, but he wanted Loki to have everything he needed, so he rolled out of bed. Loki owlishly blinked up at him and gestured at him to come back, but Sam had something to do first.

"Strip," he ordered.

"I normally wouldn't say no to sex, but I'm exhausted," Loki said.

It was the first time Sam had heard him sound so hesitant. "We're not having sex."

Loki cocked his head. "Why not? Please tell me you don't believe you'll hurt the baby if you fuck me."

"I know I wouldn't." But he couldn't say it didn't weird him out just a bit. He'd get used to it, though. There was no way he was staying away from Loki for the rest of the pregnancy. "But since we're going to be in bed for the next twelve or so hours, I want both of us to be comfortable. Wouldn't you feel better if you showered and put on some of my clothes instead of your jeans?" They were tight, which Sam usually enjoyed because it gave him a great view of Loki's ass, but there was no way they were comfortable to sleep in.

"But I don't want to get up again," Loki whined.

"I'll shower with you and even wash you."

Like Sam had hoped, that was enough incentive for Loki to haul himself out of bed. They dragged themselves into the bathroom, and Sam undressed both of them after turning on the water. Loki sagged against him as he washed him, and

Sam couldn't avoid looking the truth in the eyes — or as it was, in the stomach. He hadn't noticed it before, but there *was* a slight bump on Loki's stomach. He'd never have associated it with a baby, but his child was growing there, and he couldn't stop himself from cupping his hand around it.

"That's your child," Loki whispered.

Sam kissed him. "It's *our* child." Sam had never thought about having children and becoming a father, but for Loki and their baby, he'd be the best partner and dad anyone could ever want.

Epilogue

Loki squeezed Sam's hand and resisted the urge to scream. Sam was already frantic enough without Loki adding to it, and Loki tried to remind himself that he'd already been through this. It wasn't the first time he gave birth, and it might not be the last if Sam wanted other children.

At the moment, Loki didn't.

His entire stomach hardened as a contraction tore through it. He pressed the back of his head against the pillow and stared at the ceiling, gritting his teeth. He panted through the pain, vaguely listening to Taweret telling him to push. She'd taken over from Toth once Loki's pregnancy had reached its end, and Loki was relieved he hadn't needed to rely on anyone from his own pantheon. He still had friends there, but he felt much more comfortable with Egyptian gods.

He pressed his feet into the mattress and tried to obey, but his body didn't want to answer. He was exhausted, and he needed this to be over.

A warm hand stroked his forehead. "You can do it," Sam murmured.

Loki looked him in the eyes. He wanted to give up, but Sam wouldn't allow that. Besides, what could he do? He needed to see this through, whether he liked it or not. "We're not having any more children," he told Sam.

Sam laughed and kissed Loki's knuckles. "Whatever you say. How about you get this baby out first?"

Loki swallowed and looked down at his stomach. It was still swollen, but it wouldn't be for long. As soon as the baby was out, Loki was turning his body back to what it had been before, and this time, he'd make sure there was no baby-making equipment in it.

He felt the next contraction surge, and when he looked at Sam, Sam nodded. Loki sucked in a breath, squeezed Sam's hand, and allowed the contraction to take over. This time, when Taweret told him to push, he did.

He felt something move between his legs, then an incredible pressure. Then, finally, it disappeared, and Taweret was holding a screaming baby. Loki slumped back onto the pillow and panted, relieved it was over. His body was still in pain, and Taweret would no doubt want to check that everything was okay before Loki put everything back into place, but he was done with the hardest part.

"It's a boy," Taweret said, smiling down at the baby she was wrapping in a white sheet.

Loki and Sam had already been aware of that. A few days after they'd come home from the cave, Toth had contacted them to tell them that the barley Loki had peed on had sprouted. Apparently, that meant he was having a boy, but Loki hadn't quite believed it until Sam had taken him to a human doctor. The woman had been shocked to see Loki pregnant, but she hadn't dared say anything about it, and she'd given him an ultrasound. She'd confirmed he was carrying a boy, and while Loki hadn't cared whether he was having a boy or girl, he was relieved to find out everything looked the way they should.

Sam let go of Loki's hand and took a step toward Taweret. He paused before reaching them and turned back to Loki, but Loki waved him away. "Go meet our son," he whispered.

Sam's eyes were wide and damp looking as he obeyed. He approached Taweret as if she might throw the baby at him and run away, but of course, she didn't. She continued cleaning the child, allowing Sam to come closer and gently touch a tiny fist.

"He's here," Sam whispered.

"He is, and everything is as it should be," Taweret said. "Congratulations, Dads."

Loki briefly closed his eyes. He'd done it. He'd given Sam a child, and he couldn't have been happier.

He and Sam had slowly worked things out over the past few months. In the beginning, they'd both stayed in Sam's room in the apartment he shared with his best friends, but it had been obvious there wouldn't be enough space for the three of them once the baby was born. They'd visited all of Loki's homes around the world, and eventually, they'd settled on one that was in the same city where Sam lived. That way, he could be close to his friends, who he was already calling Uncle Arlo and Aunt Kimberly, and the baby would grow up with them in his life.

It was odd for Loki to have so many people in his family. He was related to most of the Norse gods by blood, but most of them had never seemed like they cared. Loki had only started to understand what it was to have a family after he'd met Nu and Qebui, and now he wouldn't have it any other way. It was better to have his own family that he'd built, with people who cared about him and wanted him to be happy, than having one that was related to him by blood but couldn't care less.

A hand on his knee made him jerk back, and he realized he'd been falling asleep. Taweret stood next to him, her arms empty, and Loki panicked for a moment before he saw that Sam was holding their son.

"I'll give you a quick checkup," Taweret said. She poked around Loki's lower body while he did his best to ignore it and focus on Sam. He couldn't look away from Sam and the way he was holding their baby. He knew Sam had been worried that he wouldn't know what to do once the baby was born and that he wouldn't be a good father, and Loki had spent the past few months reassuring him.

As long as he tried being a good dad, and as long as he loved their child, he'd be great as a parent. Even now, he was looking down at their son, cooing at him and gently stroking his cheek. Loki couldn't see much of the baby, just a shock of black hair over his forehead, but he waited until Taweret was done with him and he was back to his normal self to get up from the bed and join his family.

Sam looked up when he heard him, and he frowned. "Shouldn't you still be in bed?"

"I'm fine."

"You just gave birth."

"And I'm a god, so as soon as Taweret said everything looked good, I took care of it." Loki raised an arm and squeezed his bicep to make Sam laugh. "I'm as good as new. I'm tired, but I promise I'm great. Besides, I want to meet our son."

Sam's cheeks flushed. "I'm sorry I've been hogging him."

"You're his father. I'm not offended or anything. I wanted you to have these first few moments with him, and I'm glad you did."

But now it was Loki's turn, and when Sam gently gave him the baby, he took him.

He looked down at his son. Just as he'd seen earlier, the baby had black hair already growing on top of his head. His eyes were closed, and he seemed to be sleeping, as if the birth had exhausted him. Loki could understand that. They both needed rest, but he doubted they'd get much of it, at least not for the next few moments.

"I suppose everyone is still out there," he said.

Taweret chuckled. She was moving around the room, setting everything to rights as she was no doubt used to. Loki wasn't the first godly birth she'd attended. "They'll be barging in as soon as you tell them the baby is here. Make sure to sit down before you do so and kick them out if you're too tired. Even though you're a god, you just gave birth, and you deserve not only rest, but also time on your own to bond with your son."

Loki and Sam looked at each other. "What do you want me to do?" Sam asked.

"You should let them in. I'm going to do as Taweret ordered and sit down. And please, make sure Frigg is the first to come in."

Sam nodded and kissed his cheek. He hesitated, then he kissed the baby's forehead. He still looked bewildered, but Loki suspected that was the case with every parent. Sam had gotten used to the thought of becoming a dad over the past few months, and he'd been incredible as he supported Loki through the pregnancy. He still had normal doubts about being a father, but they'd be fine.

Loki had just settled down in the bed when the door opened again. Sam stepped in, gently guiding Frigg forward. She was hesitant, but she smiled when she saw Loki and the baby. "I'm glad to see everything went well," she said.

More people walked into the room behind her, but Loki ignored them. He gestured at Frigg to come closer, and she did. When she reached them, Loki smiled at her. "This is my son, Hodr."

Frigg jerked away. She looked at Loki with wide eyes that were already filling with tears. "You're calling him Hodr?"

"We hesitated between Hodr and Baldur, but we thought Hodr would be good. I'll always be sorry I couldn't save him."

"You tried, and you're one of the few. Thank you for this." She pulled herself up. "This baby is under my protection. Whatever happens, whoever he becomes, he always will be. Anyone who tries hurting him will have to go through me."

Loki was getting emotional, which was the one thing he'd hoped to avoid. He should have known better.

Once Frigg was done fussing over the baby, more people took her place. Jimmy was there, along with Qebui, as well as Sed, his king, Nu, and, surprisingly, Ra. Loki hadn't told anyone from his pantheon except Frigg that he was giving birth, but he would. He still had a few friends there, and he wanted them to know about it.

But he was relieved when everyone finally left, and he, Sam, and Hodr were alone. He stayed in bed, and Sam settled next to him, wrapping an arm around his shoulder and bringing him and Hodr close. The night was falling, and Loki had never been happier.

He'd never thought any of this would happen when he'd first noticed Sam at the club, but he was glad he hadn't given up on wooing him. He had everything he'd never known he wanted. Sam had been Loki's unlikely savior in more ways than one, and Loki wouldn't have it any different.

About the Author

Catherine is the creator of several series, most of them paranormal, including the Whitedell Pride Series and the Gillham Pack Series. While she graduated in translation, she decided to go the writer's way because it was more fun to create her own stories and characters.

She's been living in Italy for more than twenty years, but she's a daughter of the North—Belgium to be precise—and she misses it so much that she's already planning to move back.

She loves pizza—probably too much—her son, her pets, and of course, books. She sneaks some reading time into her schedule every time she has five minutes free from writing, demands from her various pets and son, and lastly, housework.

Connect with her:

lievens.catherine@gmail.com
BookBub: https://www.bookbub.com/authors/catherine-lievens
Website: https://authorcatherinelievens.com/
Facebook: https://www.facebook.com/catherine.lievens.9
Facebook Group: https://www.facebook.com/groups/411788002341528/
Twitter: https://twitter.com/authorCLievens
Newsletter: http://eepurl.com/c-uvKn